DEATH RIDES THE RIO

DEATH RIDES THE RIO

JACKSON COLE

WHEELER
CHIVERS

This Large Print edition is published by Wheeler Publishing, Waterville, Maine, USA and by AudioGO Ltd, Bath, England.
Wheeler Publishing, a part of Gale, Cengage Learning.

LIBRARY OF CONGRESS CATALOGING-IN-PUBLICATION DATA

Cole, Jackson.
    Death rides the Rio / by Jackson Cole. — Large print ed.
        p. cm. — (Wheeler Publishing large print Western)
    ISBN-13: 978-1-4104-3726-6 (pbk.)
    ISBN-10: 1-4104-3726-4 (pbk.)
    1. Large type books. I. Title.
PS3505.O2685D44 2011
813'.52—cdc22   2011005119

BRITISH LIBRARY CATALOGUING-IN-PUBLICATION DATA AVAILABLE

Published in 2011 in the U.S. by arrangement with Golden West Literary Agency.
Published in 2011 in the U.K. by arrangement with Golden West Literary Agency.

U.K. Hardcover: 978 1 445 83748 2 (Chivers Large Print)
U.K. Softcover: 978 1 445 83749 9 (Camden Large Print)

Printed in the United States of America
1 2 3 4 5 6 7 15 14 13 12 11

DEATH RIDES THE RIO

CHAPTER I
MASSACRE

High up in the *sierras* Death crouched close at hand ready to leap upon its victims. For, deep in the wild fastness of the Southwest country, with its breath-taking majestic sweeps, terror stalked.

But the vast land remained untouched by the knowledge that a dread presence was marring its beauty. The grama grass and the feathery huisache with its yellow flower-heads exuded its overpowering fragrance. The scrubby floor-growth flourished amid the chaparral covering the grey hills, that stood like sentinels in an army line.

The cactus flats abounded in the deep valleys where ran the lean *caporal* birds. And the mesquite ridges were filled with myriad insects and gorgeously hued butterflies that hummed in the hot yellow sunlight, watched by the unwinking, beady eyes of the deadly snakes. To the south the Rio Grande showed, a winding, shifting, silver ribbon.

The variety of cactus was amazing: cholla with its single thick stem for many feet, from which curved branches like the deformed arms of the tortured; prickly-pear and cat-claw; tall, white ocotillo wands. The thirty-foot high green-yellow mesquite was flowering with star blooms as white as snowflakes.

The land looked as though the foot of man had never profaned its solemn, brooding peace. But death waited close at hand.

Something moved in a deeply cut pass. It was a wash, dry at the time, with high walls of crumbling rock that here and there formed a steep slide. It widened at the top in a series of ledges, like the steps of a giant's stairway.

Through the arroyo came a long, twisting line of laden mules. *Aparejos,* baskets that were shaped to fit snugly around their barrel sides, strapped beneath each belly, creaked with the slow, plodding motion of the animals. These aparejos were filled with bulky goods, and a sun-ray caught and glittered on the end of a dull silver bar whose wrapping had fallen.

The mounted drivers rode mustangs, trimmed with the accoutrements those of Spanish descent so enjoy, spangles and little bells, velvets and braids. Rifles rode slung in leather loops; six-shooters in studded belts, long knives in sheaths. They were Mexican peons.

But their leader was a don, of hidalgo blood. His face was sensitive, intelligent. His large and dark eyes were filled with pride of noble descent. He wore a steeple sombrero and there were silver buttons on his bell trousers, a scarlet serape at his slim waist.

The train was moving northward through the pass. The crunch of stones under the moving hoofs and the creak of leather, came faintly through the warm, drowsy air.

A voice that seemed the quintessence of brutal evil suddenly shrieked: "NOW!"

Without further warning, from both sides of the narrow way in which the Mexican packtrain was trapped, rose up bandanna-masked men, eyes gleaming with ferocity above their disguise. They had been hidden on the ledges along the steep canyon sides, awaiting their prey, which had come at last.

The sun glinted on the smooth rifle barrels as they were swung down on the Mexicans. The cracking explosions swelled to the volume of a fusillade. The peons began to fall, screaming.

The don jerked on the rein of his fine mustang, and the animal reared backward as he swung. His handsome face showed no fear as he ripped out his pistol and coolly fired back at the killers he could glimpse hanging over the ledges.

"Fight, men," he shouted in Spanish.

Ten peons had slumped in their saddles at the first murderous volley. The shrieks of the wounded rose, punctuating the din. The panicky mules and horses lashed out with sharp hoofs, disturbing the aim of the few Mexicans able to draw their guns. The bucking animals bumped each other in the narrow way, unable to free themselves in the crush.

"Save us, Don Luis, save us," a despairing peon cried to the leader.

Don Luis could fight and die like a Spanish gentleman. He took aim at a yellow Stetson crown boldly thrust over a ledge, and pulled his trigger. The hat flew off and a man yelped as his hair was parted by the bullet, blood spurting up from the scalp.

"Get him — get that rat," roared the voice of the boss above.

Concentrated lead death tore into the don, as gun muzzles swung upon him. He was dead before he slid from his high-pronged saddle, and was trampled under the slashing hoofs of the maddened beasts.

There was no way out. There was no

mercy. The gunfire continued, a torture-some death beat a tattoo that did not allow any man in the train to escape its call. The cries diminished, for a few of the Mexicans remained to ask mercy.

A couple of the pack-train riders who had been in the drag of the cavalcade managed to swing as they saw how hopeless their cause was; they tried to burst from the pass but men were posted to prevent that. Cruel faces, half-hidden by the masks, in which the Mexicans read their doom, showed a few yards above and with a final despairing shriek the peons felt the stab of eternity.

The masked man who had directed the awful massacre from the safety of his high perch, stared down into the smoking desolation that was the work of his twisted brain. None of the fifty Mexicans of the train could speak now, though a few, sorely wounded, groaned beneath the bodies of their comrades and animals.

"Down in there and finish 'em all off," he growled. "I don't want any rats creepin' back and squealing."

Sweat poured down the bronzed brows of the tough gunmen who carefully made their way around into the canyon of death.

"Get that silver out," snapped the chief. "Monty, you clumsy fool, careful of that other stuff, it'll break."

The arch murderer made his way through the mess by literally walking on the dead or dying bodies of his victims. A peon with great dark eyes, face contorted in awful agony, shifted a little as the chief paused near him.

"Mercy — in God's name, spare me, señor," he gasped in Spanish. "I have three little ones and —"

The masked leader raised the six-shooter in his hand, calmly drew back the spurred hammer, aimed at the peon's face and raised his thumb. The firing-pin hit the cartridge and the big slug tore into the Mexican's brain.

"Finish 'em all," he snarled, teeth clicking.

Scattered shots told his orders were being carried out. Gunmen rooted in the masses of flesh for any still able to writhe, putting despatching bullets into them.

A red haze rose from the blood-soaked pass.

High in the brassy sky tiny black specks grew larger as the buzzards swooped down; they seemed to have watched the murderers, preparing their gruesome feast. They would, with their friends the coyotes, have a wild dance that night.

The leader made a hurried survey of the baskets. He pulled the covers from several packages.

"Just what I wanted," he muttered. To a squat hombre nearby he said, "Stumpy, bring up our horses. Tell Dave to pack everything as it stands. This is only the beginning."

Not a hundred miles north of the death pass, Buck Stamford, line rider for the ME Connected Ranch, which ran many thousands of steers in huge Brewster County, pulled up his mustang and stared from the rise he had just topped. His weather-beaten face showed his astounded amazement.

"Well, dang my sandpaper hide!" he growled, and drove a spur rowel into his pony's flank.

He came quickly up with the small herd of ME Connected cows that was being driven south by a quartet of riders. They did not appear at all excited as Buck rode in. The leader was a giant, broad as a bull in the body, with a heavy head of brown hair, blue eyes with a cross-shaped scar, livid against his tanned skin, that ran from under the matted black brow to his left temple. Evidently some enemy in the past had slashed him there with a knife. He rode a great horse to carry his weight, crossed gunbelts on his mighty chest.

The four riders swung on Buck and surveyed him calmly. The giant gazed intently at him without even a break in the chewing of his tobacco.

"Hey, what the hell's the idee?" roared Buck hotly. "Them's our cows."

The big hombre grinned, showing a gap where one of his yellow buck teeth had been knocked out, perhaps in the same fracas when he had received the knife mark.

"They're our'n now, waddy," he replied carelessly.

"I'll shoot yore ears off," a slight, evil-faced rustler snarled, from the line rider's other flank. Buck saw him digging for his pistol, and the cowboy's tanned hand swiftly dropped to the butt of his six-gun to defend himself, as he turned his body that way.

At that instant the giant, displaying amazing speed despite his size, made a draw-fire with his .45, putting a bullet through Stamford from side to side. The line rider coughed blood, and sprawled on his pony's neck.

The mustang bucked and threw off his dying rider, galloped away. Smeared on his saddle and hide was a wide splotch of blood. Buck lay doubled in the dirt, twitching.

"Put a rope on that and drag it into the bushes," ordered the big fellow, as he turned back to hazing the steers, without another look at the dying man.

CHAPTER II
RANGER BLOOD

Ranger Lon Martin was dusty and dry from the hundreds of miles ridden from Texas Ranger headquarters. He had been despatched by Captain Bill McDowell in reply to urgent complaints of murder and rustling in Brewster. He pulled into the town late at night.

During the last few hours of his ride, he had had for his guide the twinkling lights of the cowtown on the railroad. McDowell, who had charge of policing a Texas section bigger than most countries, had ordered Ranger Martin to clean up Brewster and catch the murderer of the ME Connected line-rider, Buck Stamford.

The big saloon on the east side of the plaza was wide open. Martin left his pony at the livery stable up the road for a big feed and careful grooming, and strolled over to the place. He was stiff-legged from his days of riding, throat dry as desert sand.

"Shore'll be good to moisten it with a real drink," he told himself. The lukewarm water from his canteen had only kept him from dying of thirst; it was scarcely a pleasure to swallow.

As he cut over toward the big saloon, two gunshots crackled inside. A momentary silence followed, then excited cries filled the quiet night. A huge man strolled from the doorway right into Martin.

The big fellow's eyes were still partially blinded from the lights inside and he had failed to see the Ranger till he collided with him. He cursed and did his best to swing his six-gun on Martin.

"No yuh don't!" snapped Martin as he brought his sturdy fist in a short but stiff uppercut that drove the gunman's teeth together. As the gunman's head snapped back between his shoulder blades Martin's left hand thrust aside the pistol arm and the slug from it drove into the porch boards, barely singeing the Ranger's boot. Then Martin's own Colt rammed into the giant's side ribs.

"Back inside, or fresh air'll irrigate yore belly," growled Martin.

"Damn yuh — yuh'll die for this," rasped the prisoner.

16

Martin gave him a shove that started him through the wide doorway. Those who had ducked for cover when the shooting started, had emerged, gathered in a crowd about the corpse of a short man flat on his back near the footrail of the bar. There was a bullet hole from the left temple to the right.

"What happened?" demanded Martin, keeping an eye on the scar-faced, glowering hombre he had captured.

"Say, that big galoot shot him jest on account he didn't like his voice," cried a witness.

"He didn't," snapped a cold, sharp voice. "I saw it all. It was self-defense."

"Why'd this feller run, then?" asked Martin.

"Who asked yuh to come hornin' in here?" snarled the big captive.

"I'm a Ranger," Martin said bluntly slapping down his badge on the bar. The silver star set on a silver circle gleamed menacingly.

No one made any more objections. Ranger Martin stared at the huge man, read the fierce hatred in the blood-flecked killer's eyes, one of which was half shut by the drawn flesh of a jagged knife-scar.

"Yuh're arrested for murder," drawled Martin. "I'll lock yuh up for the night." Addressing the bartender from the corner of his seamed mouth, he asked that semi-official: "Anybuddy at the jail to open up?"

"Marshal Davis is away till tomorrer, but his depitty's on guard at the hoosegow," replied the barkeeper.

Most of the loungers in the saloon, cowboys in off the range, freighters who drove mule-teams across the mountains to the interior, gamblers and riffraff, trailed in the Ranger's wake. Martin, a cocked six-gun at the big man's spine, paraded him to the north end of the Plaza to the adobe jail. It was a strong building with three-foot baked brick walls and inch-wide steel bars. There was a lank, tobacco-chewing deputy in charge, who let Martin in. They shoved the murderer into a square cell in the rear half of the place.

"I'll be along in the mornin' to see 'bout him," promised Martin. "Want to talk to Marshal Davis, too. I understand the ME Connected's had some rustler trouble."

"Shore has, Ranger. We bin so busy we jest run in circles."

Martin, leaving the giant gunman securely locked in for the night, returned to the saloon to enjoy his belated drink. He was a good-looking man of forty, one of McDow-ell's steadiest and most experienced officers. As he drank, he drew out the bartender on the shooting affray, learning that the killing had been pointless, a wanton gesture of a drunken, too-sure gunman.

"I've seen that big galoot quite a bit lately," the barkeep informed Martin. "He's got lots of friends hereabouts. They don't seem to work much — at least, not at anything honest."

Martin nodded. He was down here to clean the Brewster district of such characters. The town marshal might be efficient and honest, but he had his hands full keeping order in the immediate vicinity, policing the settlement.

When he had finished eating, Martin yawned widely. He felt the need for sleep after his long ride. He looked around for a likely place to sleep. Then he went to the stable. Here was as good as anywhere in this kind of town. He got out his warsack with his blankets, and rolling himself up in a pile of hay under a shed in the rear yard, he was soon asleep.

He woke to the clutch of powerful hands on his throat. He tried to struggle but was held down, pinned by the knees of many men, he was unable to move his limbs. His eyes bulged from the pressure on his windpipe, and words were choked in his throat.

"You slugs are a damn nuisance," a brutal voice growled in his ear. "Well, yuh're one who won't arrest any more of my pals and interfere with my plans. Here, Dude, here's his little star-badge. Yuh're it. You're slick enough looking, and in the morning we'll take Mike out of that lousy jail."

The last words Ranger Martin heard before going to his final reward were the lurid curses of the boss. The latter stooped, and drove a long, sharp knife under his ribs into his heart. Death touched him and eternal darkness closed down on a hardy veteran of the Texas Rangers.

Early the following morning a slim, rugged-looking young man rode up to Brewster jail and dismounted. Marshal Cal Davis had just come on duty, allowing his deputy to go home. The sun was still ruby-red in the sky, and but few citizens were yet out of their blanket-rolls.

"Mornin', Marshal," said the young rider cheerfully. "How's my pris'ner behavin'?"

Davis regarded him. "The on'y pris'ner we got here is Gila Mike Turner," he said slowly. "Leastways, that's what I learned he's called. Who are yuh?"

"Why — I'm Ranger Tom Thorpe, Martin's ridin' mate. Here's my star." He laid the badge on the desk for a moment. "Martin done rode over to the ME Connected to see Milton English, the boss there, 'bout that rustlin' trouble. Figger this Gila Mike, as yuh call him, may know somethin' of it, and mebbe the ME riders kin identify him."

The Ranger badge, the smooth flow of words which were so logical, the clean appearance of the man, left Davis with no doubts at all. He rose, taking the cell keys from a locked desk drawer.

"Okay, Ranger. Yuh fellers took him so I guess yuh got a right to do with him as yuh see fit."

The giant Gila Mike, head in his mighty paws, sat despondently on the hard bench inside the cell. He glowered at Davis, but his eyes flickered an instant as he saw the other man at the marshal's heels. Davis opened the barred gate.

"Yuh got handcuffs?" asked Davis. "This hombre's one tough nut, I figger."

"Shore, shore!" The smooth young man snapped cuffs on the gunman's beefy wrists. "Much obliged, Marshal, see yuh later. Martin oughta be back this afternoon."

Then he returned to his prisoner and said coldly, "C'mon yuh gun-totin' coyote."

Davis watched with approval the care the young man took as he mounted, keeping

Gila Mike, handcuffed to the saddle-horn, under a ready six-gun.

But the big prisoner was very tractable, to Davis's surprise. His thick lips were pursed, and the half-closed eyes gave him a perpetual appearance of rascality, but he made no attempt to escape.

Davis now stood in the jail doorway, watching them ride up the dusty road and head out onto the northern grazing plains in the direction of the ME Connected.

Once out of sight and hearing of town, safe in the bush, the youth unlocked the handcuffs, freeing Gila Mike, who uttered an explosive sigh of relief.

"Phew," he growled, "thought they had me that time, Dude!"

"It worked!" cried Dude, laughing uproariously. "The boss said it would, and danged if it didn't!"

"But how'd yuh git rid of that Ranger?" demanded Turner, shaking his great body in his new found freedom.

Dude winked, made a gesture signifying the driving of a knife. "I got to laugh when I think how the marshal'll feel when they dig that corpse out from the hayrack!"

Chapter III
The Lone Wolf Rides

Ranger Jim Hatfield, known by reputation throughout the thousand-mile width of Texas as the "Lone Wolf," strode into the office of Cap'n Bill McDowell.

McDowell's fierce old brows were touching, in a frown that meant trouble for someone who had seen fit to defy the law. It was said of McDowell that he would charge hell with a bucket of water — and what's more, he had done it, and put out the conflagration on more than one occasion.

The captain of the Rangers shook the communication he gripped in his gun-gnarled hand. Then he surveyed the mighty young man who waited before him, the body lines having all the grace of a panther.

Jim Hatfield was well over six feet tall, broad chest tapering to the lean hips and waist of the fighting man's figure. At the end of his long arms hung thin but strong, wiry hands capable of blinding speed and accuracy, with a six-gun, or in hand-to-hand combat. Those hands could tear out an adversary's throat with their viselike grip.

The Ranger's grey-green eyes, shaded by long black lashes, were calm. But McDowell knew how, in battle, they clouded up, darkened like a fair summer sky when shrouded by a thunderstorm. The rugged features were made pleasant by a good-humored mouth which fronted the tight sweep of the fighting jaw.

He was the Lone Wolf, the terror of deadly lawbreakers throughout the length and breadth of Texas.

"Yes, suh, Cap'n," drawled Hatfield. "Yuh sent for me?" The voice was, like a tombstone, quiet, steady, but it could be hard as eternal granite when necessary.

"Hatfield, Ranger Martin's dead, murdered. In this here letter, Marshal Davis of Brewster — Martin done rode down there on patrol — claims Martin arrested a gunman named Gila Mike Turner in the saloon, for a shootin'. Here's the rub: Martin left his pris'ner in the town jail fer the night, but hear this: 'The other Ranger, Thorpe, claimed the pris'ner Gila Mike, took him out of my custody!' Now Martin was down there alone, the on'y Ranger within two hundred miles. And there *ain't any Ranger Thorpe.*"

"Must've been some pard of Gila Mike posed as a Ranger."

"Mebbe so. We can't 'low sech. There ain't never bin so many Rangers, Hatfield, not over a couple hundred at a time, since the

Mexican War. But every one is wuth a passel of ordinary fellers. And why? 'Cause we take care of our own, and that's the reason the Rangers kin handle sich a big chunk of hell as the Southwest's bin made by various tough hombres itchin' to try their quickdraw against the law.

"We git the jump on 'em and don't let 'em roll. Our hull power rests in a Ranger bein' able to handle as many skunks as may come against him. Martin's killers must be taken, made to pay the price.

"Seems to me that big slice of land wants some careful lookin' into. The ME Connected Ranch, which runs that range, claims a line rider of theirs was kilt and they've lost sev'ral bunches of cows. That's why Martin done rode there. Hatfield, yuh got a rovin' commission to clean up Brewster and vicinity, and ketch Martin's murderers. When yuh get there see Cal Davis, he's okay, an old friend of mine and dead honest."

Ranger Hatfield saluted. The rugged face did not change its set expression, though McDowell noted the darkening of the greygreen eyes. Martin and Hatfield had ridden together and fought side by side on previous occasions, enjoyed themselves as two such men will between jobs.

McDowell had snapped off that invisible leash which released this force for good against the minions of evil.

McDowell watched him as the Ranger started out to his big sorrel, Goldy, who playfully nipped at his mighty master's sleeve. The Lone Wolf patted the golden horse's neck.

"Him and that cayuse are two of a kind. Tough as tanned leather and on'y half-tamed," muttered Cap'n Bill. "Hatfield don't have much more to say than the hoss, but he shore brings home the bacon, yessir, he brings it home all cured and ready to fry.

"I'd dislike bein' the hombres he's headed fer. I never see the man who could match him fer speed of hand and brain. And as fer nerves — he's got as many as a tombstone!"

Goldy was in fine fettle, well rested, ready to carry Hatfield on his dangerous mission. In a saddle sling rode the Ranger's rifle; he had on two six-guns in oiled holsters that were pliable and broken in, so there would be no drag in drawing them. A small war-sack completed his kit.

Hatfield swung a long leg across the high Western saddle. Like most cayuses, Goldy had to enjoy a little buck to warm himself up, and the Ranger let him run as he wished

26

for a mile. Then the sorrel settled down to his pace-consuming trot, headed for the Southwest county.

Silently they rode toward a land of murder and gigantic crime, where death threatened at every step, where the Lone Wolf would be a lone wolf indeed, fighting almost impossible odds. Had Cap'n Bill McDowell knows into what he was ordering his star officer, he might have been inclined to send all his two hundred Rangers along to help.

At dark they camped and slept. Day after day they rode, the handsome sorrel carrying his rider nearer and nearer tall trouble. It was a warm afternoon when they finished a record-time trip, with Brewster in sight.

The town lay eastward of the Guadalupes, the land rolling prairie between the rugged mountains. Several outfits grazed in the county but the ME Connected was the largest. The town was a cow-loading stop on the Rio Grande and Eastern, the main street split by the tracks.

Brewster was a typical Border town. Frame and adobe buildings, some with false second-story fronts, others leaned against one another as though weary of the strain of standing in the sun's baking heat. Teams were drawn up, with the horses hanging their heads over the hitch-racks. Saddled ponies stood awaiting their masters who walked along the sidewalks which were awninged with wood.

There were two or three substantial structures, one the jail, the other a good-sized bank built of stone, and the large saloon. A large, square plaza occupied the center of town, the saloon on the east, down toward the tracks, the bank on the west. The jail was up at the northern edge of the central square.

The trail Hatfield was on ran along the railroad tracks until it reached the station, where it branched into Main Street. The station was simply a small open-front shed. Down the track were corrals with loading chutes.

And there on a siding, as Goldy stepped past on the sandy dirt, lifting his knees high in his pride, Hatfield noted the private railway car which the through express had disdainfully paused to discard.

On the rear platform sat a very pretty young woman, smiling at a lean young fellow with tanned, serious face, dark hair and broad shoulders. The girl was glowingly pretty, of healthy blond beauty, hair very light in the sun. The roses in her cheeks, her white teeth that showed as she smiled, her deep-blue eyes, entranced the young man, who was dressed in a khaki outfit and leather boots.

Baggage had been unloaded from the car. There were pack mules drowsily waiting around, with supply boxes, too. Among the equipment stood a sloppy looking, middle-aged fat man with a grey-spattered, golden Van Dyke beard, and a frowning face; the lenses of his glasses were so thick they distorted his wrinkled eyes. There was a tall fellow, rather slim, with him, a man with a mobile, intelligent face, white teeth showing under a tiny black dude's mustache. As he spoke with the fat man he gave the impression of great efficiency.

There were watering troughs nearby, and Goldy, throat dry from his long run, headed for one. As the sorrel drank, the Ranger slung a muscular leg around his saddle horn, rolling a cigarette; his grey-green eyes scrutinized the party.

The tall man seemed to resent this, for he frowned, and waved Hatfield off.

"Run along, waddy," he ordered. "We don't need any more help, and we don't welcome snoopers."

The stout man stared at the big Ranger, too, still frowning.

Hatfield did not bother to answer the slim

man. He waited till Goldy had drunk his fill, and then swung on to the main street of Brewster. He found that the jail, at the far end of the big plaza, was locked up.

Hatfield decided he must get the lay of the land, and the town saloon was as good a spot as any for that. The Ranger followed his usual policy — to all intents and purposes he was a wandering waddy.

He left Goldy at the stable, then crossed the road and ducked under the hitch-rack, beneath the wooden awning into the saloon. It was quiet in the place, not many men in yet. He guessed it was too early. The Ranger nodded to the bartender and ordered a drink.

After a time, as dusk settled over the land, he went into an annex and sat down to eat his dinner. When the town marshal showed up, Hatfield would take him to a corner where they could talk unobserved; thus he would learn what facts Davis had in his possession about the matters interesting to the Ranger.

Hatfield did not wish to warn any criminal element in the vicinity that a Ranger was in town. They would at once guess, if they were guilty of Martin's murder, the purpose of his visit, and might leave the neighborhood before he identified them.

The restaurant and hotel annex to the saloon had two doors, one that led into the huge bar, and another directly on the street. Hatfield had taken a table by the front window, and could see the plaza. The party from the private car on Brewster siding, the fat man and the one who had resented the Ranger's presence, the young man with the girl on his arm, and two more evident Easterners, one a little wizened man of fifty, another a large fellow with a red face and strong eyes, strolled along the walk, evidently looking at the sights. The girl and her escort crossed the road, while the four others entered the saloon.

Thudding of hoofs in the road, swirls of dust rising as riders cantered up in style, grew more frequent. Cowboys were coming to the bar for the evening's fun, and townspeople had finished supper and were making tracks for the cow-town's center of amusement.

In the glass the Ranger saw a stocky man with a five-pointed marshal's star pinned to his blue vest, seamed face wrinkled with worry. He rose and stepped to the street door.

"Marshal Davis?" Hatfield's voice was low and compelling.

The officer stopped in his stride, slowly

turning, looking questioningly at the big Lone Wolf.

"Yes, suh. What kin I do fer yuh?"

"Come on in and take a cup o' cawfee."

Davis entered, sat down opposite the Ranger, who was leisurely finishing his ham and eggs.

"McDowell sent me," Hatfield told him in a soft drawl, "to ketch the sidewinders who kilt Martin." He silently shoved the letter Davis had written McDowell across the table; that would prove to the marshal that he was honest.

"I'm shore sorry 'bout Martin," the old lawman said slowly. "I ain't had any luck ketchin' them buzzards." He shook his head sadly. "What's yore name, son?"

"Hatfield — Jim Hatfield."

Davis whistled, and new respect came into his sun-wrinkled eyes. "I've heard tell of yuh, Hatfield. It's a pleasure to meet yuh" — his hand shot out — "be glad to do anything I kin to help."

"Tell me what yuh know 'bout Martin."

"Well," began the lawman, "Martin arrested an hombre known as Gila Mike Turner. Gila Mike's bin tearin' 'round these parts fer some time, but he never got caught redhanded before. The only reason Martin caught up with him was because he was likkered up that night, and he done shot a man he didn't like the looks of, jest a wanton play.

"Martin caught him as he come out and dragged him to the calaboose. My depitty was there, took the pris'ner in. Next mornin', a smooth young feller comes along with a Texas Ranger's badge, says he's Martin's pardner and he wants Gila Mike fer legal purposes. So I deliver Turner, and they ride off.

"That's the last I see of 'em, but next day a pony pushed back some hay behind the livery stable acrost the way and there was Martin's body — he had been stabbed through the heart.

"I done wrote McDowell of it. I got plenty troubles, what with Milton English of the ME Connected yellin' my ear sore 'bout the rustlin' goin' on lately, and the killin' of his line rider, Buck Stamford. County Sheriff's bin down but he's got so much ground to cover it takes all his time jest ridin' around!"

"What's this Gila Mike look like?"

"A giant, weighs two-thirty anyways, but is fast as he's huge. Got a missin' front buck tooth and a cross-shaped scar over his left eye. I figger he roams the south country below here, toward the Rio Grande."

"I might take a pasear down thataway," thought Hatfield. He wanted Gila Mike. Turner must know who had killed Martin, since his "rescuer" had had Martin's Ranger star.

"Mike's one *muy malo hombre,* a killin' bull when he's on the prod," warned Davis. "Watch him if yuh meet up with him, 'cause they say no man ever beat his draw."

The hum of voices, clicking of gambling wheels, came to them from the big saloon, as they drank their coffee.

"I'd jest as soon it wasn't known a Ranger was down here," Hatfield said. "I wanta work sorta quiet for a time."

"Right. If yuh need to do any law work, jest say yuh're one of my deputies. I bin takin' more on, tryin' to run down the killers of Buck Stamford, them rustlin' gents."

"Yuh trail any of them stolen cows?"

Davis shook his head. "No luck yit. The prairie's covered with grazin' cattle, and the chaparral and hills south of here is full of wild dogies, so tracks don't help none. I —"

He broke off suddenly as a pistol shot boomed in the saloon. The marshal shoved back his chair and ran toward the connecting door inside. But Jim Hatfield leaped the other way, onto the sidewalk, and was right outside the saloon entry.

There was yelling, cursing in the bar. Two men were backing out of the place as the silent, pantherlike Hatfield waited for them. The gunmen were busy watching the crowd inside. Through the open door, Hatfield saw the form of the red-faced Easterner, who had come in with the party from the private car on the siding.

"Stand back — that means yuh, too, Davis! Don't nobuddy show his snoot outside for ten minutes or we'll shoot it off," shouted a dark-faced, tough hombre. He and his partner put spaced shots into the bar ceiling, firing through the entry to cow the crowd.

Hatfield spoke then, quietly, but with that hint of granite in his voice:

"What's the game, boys? Kin I take a hand?"

Both startled gunmen whirled. "Take care of Davis and them inside, Phil," snapped the bigger one. He had a nose like the edge of a clam-shell, sharp, his whole face was dangerous looking. In one dirty paw he gripped a .45, hammer back under a yellow-stained thumb.

Hatfield had not drawn a gun. His long, thin hands hung limp at his sides, feet spread, steady eyes fixed on the razor-faced hombre.

"Back down, stranger. Don't want no truck with yuh, I'd jest as soon drill yuh if yuh make trouble. We ain't stoppin' fer nobuddy, savvy?"

He had swung the Colt muzzle on the Ranger, but wasn't much worried, since Hatfield's pistols were holstered. The Lone Wolf's hand flashed with the speed of light, not to his guns, which his opponent had an eye on, but to the sharp-faced fellow's wrist.

The cursing gunman let go, but the slug tore through the roof-boards instead of the big Ranger. An instant-fraction later Razor-face screamed in agony, bent to the side as Hatfield nearly broke off his fingers that were twined in the trigger guard.

Twisting the man's bones, Jim Hatfield snatched away the warm revolver. As the gunman opened his fingers and straightened up, the Ranger laid the metal barrel with a resounding smack down on the tough's forehead. The sharp-faced one folded up with a grunt at his feet.

His pal swung to shoot Hatfield. The Lone Wolf, as calmly as though performing a daily routine action, without a waste of motion, threw the pistol snatched from the other man straight into the shorter one's face. The sharp hammer spur cut the cheek, forced him, instinctively, to close his eyes an instant. In that moment Hatfield was on him like a tiger, had a gun in his side ribs. A trickle of blood started from the gunman's cheek.

"I'm leavin' yuh stand, 'cause somebuddy's gotta carry yore friend to the calaboose," drawled Hatfield.

Marshal Davis ran out, took the six-shooter from the limp hand of the second prisoner.

"Yuh rat," he growled, slapping him in the face. "Yuh shot that stranger without no warnin'. Started a scrap on purpose, the barkeeper says."

The crowd gathered about them. Davis ordered a couple of friends to keep an eye on the unconscious Razorface, and shoved the other into the saloon.

"See if he's dead," he ordered.

The blond girl, and her admirer, hearing the rumpus, came to the saloon from across the road.

"What's up?" asked the young man.

"Shootin' inside, man plugged," replied a bystander.

The girl was instantly alarmed. "Oh, Bert! I — I hope Dad's not hurt. I've got to see." She ran past Hatfield and into the bar, followed by the khaki-clad Easterner.

Hatfield waited in the doorway, watching. The man with the dude's mustache was bent over the form of the large fellow with the commanding eyes and reddish face. It was the latter who had been shot by the gunmen the Ranger had captured. Blood was pumping from a wound in his side.

"Give him air," ordered the slim man authoritatively. He was feeling for the heart beat. "He's not dead, Mr. Voorhees. But we'd better get him to bed and send for the doctor. We've gotta stop this bleeding!"

"Huh," grunted Voorhees, the fat one with the thick-lensed glasses. "Huh. He don't look like he'll be much good to us now, Vance."

Vance shook his head. "This is one professor who won't give any lectures for a while, but he'll recover."

"Oh, it's poor Dr. Jackson?" cried the young woman as she clutched Bert's arm.

"This is awful," the Easterner exclaimed. It was plain that he was greatly disturbed, as he knelt beside the silent form of Dr. Jackson.

"Selkirk, take Edith avay from dis," growled Voorhees. "Haff you no bedder sense dan to bring my dauder to see such a sight?"

Bert Selkirk flushed and straightened up. "I'll go back to the hotel and make sure they have his bed ready."

The couple brushed by Hatfield, both greatly overwrought.

"Come on to the calaboose," snapped Marshal Davis, shoving his prisoner to the porch.

"Let him tote his pal," ordered Hatfield.

Under the Lone Wolf's cool, steady gaze, the man stooped, shouldered his razor-faced friend, and staggered up the dusty road.

"If that feller back there dies," threatened Davis, keeping step behind them, "both of yuh'll swing. Why'd yuh shoot him?"

"Go to hell!" snarled the gunman over his shoulder. "Yuh kin arrest me but yuh can't make me talk."

A crowd had trailed after them to the thick-walled jail at the north side of the plaza. Jim Hatfield went inside, sat down in a chair while the marshal locked the two prisoners in a rear cell. Then Davis came in, shutting the connecting door.

"Make tracks, boys," Davis said from the doorsill to the mob, "there ain't anything more to see."

The crowd began to disperse. Most of the

men headed for the bar to wet lips made dry by excitement.

"Have a cigar," Davis said to the Ranger, and sat down in his swivel chair, across the desk from Hatfield. "That was shore a neat job yuh did, mister."

"But why'd they shoot that feller?" Hatfield wanted to know.

Davis shrugged. "Mebbe 'cause he had on dude clothes, jest didn't like his looks. That kind don't talk."

Hatfield agreed with a nod. "But they wasn't drunk, Marshal. How 'bout that bunch of pilgrims, the fat hombre and all?"

Marshal Davis shrugged. "They pulled in this mornin'. I've seed the hombre with the little mustache before, his name's George Vance. He's bin around Brewster some. But they ain't said a word as to what they're up to. They bought a bunch of trail supplies and pack animals as well as saddle hosses."

"Minin'?"

"Mebbe, or prospectin'. That fat guy's right important, it's his car and all; he must be wallowin' in money."

Hatfield ruminated. "Perfesser," he murmured aloud, "now what's a perfesser doin' out thisaway?"

"If Gila Mike ever got his hands on that fat hombre with the goat beard," Davis figured, "he'd shore be happy. Why, Gila would make him fork over every dollar he's got! It's mighty dangerous for sech pilgrims to be roamin' the chaparral."

"Yeah, but this is a free country."

"Yuh're right, and their business ain't mine, 'less 'n they break the law. Now, what —"

"Duck?" Hatfield ordered suddenly, his big body shifted, but his eyes fixed on the rectangle of the door.

Marshal Davis fell out of his chair as a bullet swirled through his hair, burning his scalp. Limp, and unconscious, he smashed heavily to the floor, and lay face down with blood staining the worn, unpainted wood.

More slugs rapped into the desk in front of Hatfield, whose six-gun was already roaring a reply to the dim figures of masked riders outside the jail, who were bunched close to the door.

CHAPTER IV
THE SOUTH TRAIL

Hatfield's brain remained as cool as glacial ice. The Ranger's heart-beat did not speed up as the heavy guns crashed, aimed to kill him and leave him a bloody, quivering pulp on the floor of the Brewster jail. It was this sheer nerve control which helped make him such a dangerous adversary in a fight, for nothing shook the perfect balance and coordination of mind and trained fighting muscles.

Crouched behind the thick oak desk, he fought back silently as was his wont. A masked man, bolder than the rest, flung himself from his saddle and leaped inside. Hatfield put a .45 slug through his brain, he crashed, twitching spasmodically on the doorway, a red spot in his forehead faintly glowing in the light of the single oil lamp.

A bullet ripped a hole through Hatfield's sombrero, another tore his shirt sleeve, others hummed past his ears. But he sent a line of lead along the center of the opening. Outside, men began to cry in pain.

Shaken by the deadly accuracy and cold nerve of the Ranger's fire, the gang jerked on their pony reins, rearing the horses back out of sight.

Hatfield jumped up and bounded to the door, gun still blaring. He leaped over the dead gunman, and was in the open.

The flashes of the guns were plainly visible in the darkness. Citizens were running from the saloon, heading for the jail at the alarm.

The pack which had attacked, broke and

rode full tilt across the plaza down Main Street. He knelt in the middle of the road, firing after the rapidly retreating riders. As they flashed past the lighted saloon, Hatfield saw among them a man extraordinarily large, mounted on a great black horse.

"Gila Mike," he guessed.

They were well out of revolver range, and sent those who had run out of the saloon scurrying for shelter by wild shooting as they rode pell-mell out of Brewster. However, some of them carried Ranger lead away with them.

There were a couple of saddled ponies at the side of the jail. Hatfield mounted one and spurred after the bunch. Crossing the railroad and leaving the buildings of the town, he found himself in the chaparral, with dust still thick in his nostrils. They had come this way, sure enough, but he could not find them in the darkness and they could dodge him forever, if they did not ambush him.

It was hopeless to search further then, so he trotted back to town and the jail. He found Marshal Davis, grunting and swearing, still dazed. He helped the lawman back into his chair.

"I callate we snaffled us a coupla Gila Mike's men," Hatfield told him.

He went to the door that led into the cells, opened it and stood looking in at the prisoners. The one he had struck over the head with his own pistol had come back to consciousness and sat slumped by his pard, rubbing his forehead.

"Yore boss jest tried to rescue yuh," he drawled.

"What yuh mean?" snarled Razorface.

"Gila Mike."

"Huh? Never heard of him. Dunno him."

"Yuh can't do nuthin' to us," cried the second. "That pilgrim ain't hurt much."

Hatfield shrugged, returned to Davis. "Uh, I shore warn't much use to yuh in that argument," grunted the marshal. "Thanks again."

"I'd like to know why they shot that perfesser," ruminated the Ranger. "These two're shore enough hooked to Gila Mike. Onlikely they'd start anything here without bein' ordered." He thought he'd like to know exactly what the purpose of the Eastern party was down there.

"I gotta have a drink, my head's splittin'," said Davis, rising on shaking legs. "C'mon."

Brewster was lively at night. Gamblers were at work in the saloons, stores brightly lighted, and honky-tonk music fanned the

44

cooling breeze off the hills. The large square plaza was filled with ponies and wagons.

As the tall Ranger strode by the stocky marshal's side, he saw the handsome Bert Selkirk across the way, and Edith Voorhees with him. Her father had left the Alhambra, the biggest place of amusement, where Professor Jackson had been wounded, and Vance, the fellow with the little mustache, had gone with him.

Davis pushed a way to the crowded bar. There were a couple of hundred men in the place, at the bar, the tables and the inside rooms, where the gamblers took the cowboys' money. Violin and piano music rose from a square dancehall.

A barkeeper shoved out whiskey to them. A big rancher, stout and tanned of face, a ten-gallon hat curved on his iron-grey head, came up and slapped the marshal on the shoulder.

"Looka here," he said sternly, "I lost more cows last night, they was drove off south and one of my men gunned and wounded. It's gotta stop. I done wrote Bill McDowell and the Texas Rangers'll clean this up if yuh can't."

"I done everything I kin, Milt," replied Davis.

The rancher glanced at the Lone Wolf.

45

"Say, ain't yuh the hombre who buffaloed them two skunks a while ago? Dang it, 'twould be my luck to miss that play! They say it was good."

"Durn right it was good," replied the marshal. "So good I asked this feller to be one of my deputies. Meet Milton English, owner of the ME Connected, Jim."

Hatfield nodded.

"Set 'em up, on me," roared English, shaking the Ranger's long hand. "Mighty glad to know a salty hombre like yourself, Jim. If yuh trace the killers of Buck Stamford I'll pay a reward outa my own pocket.

"Them steers are bein' run south; t'ain't so many it'll break me, but it makes me sore, savvy, them rustlers bin purty high-handed. We figger them beeves were run into the mountains south of here. Why, I dunno; there's no towns there."

English was a voluble man and kept on telling of his troubles.

The Ranger slept the night at Marshal Davis's home. In the morning, after breakfast, he went to the stable and threw his hulk on Goldy, who snorted his master an affectionate greeting. The big man mounted and headed south, crossing the tracks.

Plainly it was in the wild country south of

Brewster that the rustlers under Gila Mike, who were responsible for the murders of Ranger Martin and of Buck Stamford, had their hideout. It was necessary for him to have a look at the land.

Leaving the flats, along which the railway ran east and west, the trail died off into a narrow track wide enough for horses. It soon became heavily pitted with rocks, and the bush closed in. Beyond, the hills rose before him; far in the distance he saw the bald top of a mighty mountain, while to his left, on the opposite side of a narrow split, loomed another.

Goldy trotted along in the warm sunshine. The cheep of birds and hum of insects filled the air as Hatfield pushed on.

He had gone only a mile past the railroad when he saw dust ahead, and soon heard the sound of voices and the click of hoofs on the stones. Presently he came up with a small packtrain, mules laden with provisions, riders jogging along on horses. He saw Dutch Hans Voorhees, the millionaire, Edith and Selkirk. Vance was there, too, with his little black mustache, and a small wizened man who looked like another professor. Several attendants were driving the loaded mules.

Hatfield turned out to pass the train. They

all stared at him, and Vance swung his horse across Goldy's path.

"What do you want?" he demanded of the Ranger.

"Why," drawled Hatfield, with such docility in his voice that it misled Vance, "I'm jest ridin', mister."

"We don't want any spies along with us," Vance said harshly. "What takes you this way?"

"Well," replied Hatfield softly, "mebbe that's my bus'ness, jest as where yuh're headin' is yores."

He touched his Stetson to Edith Voorhees as he swung on past Vance, whose face was red with irritation. The young woman smiled at him, and Bert Selkirk nodded in a friendly fashion.

"Now what'd he mean 'bout spies," mused Hatfield, as he shoved on.

There were plenty of hoofmarks, of cattle and horses, visible to the Ranger's trained eye. Greens and yellows abounded in the chaparral. Down there somewhere must be Gila Mike Turner.

In the bottoms the earth was dry and alkaline, supporting only cactus. In the distance Hatfield saw a bunch of wild cattle staring at him from a hilltop. When he came on, they lifted their tails and headed for the bushes. He rode through the day and camped the night at the side of the trail.

It was next afternoon when they began to climb. The trail split, and Hatfield chose the left-hand fork, as it seemed more traveled, and was the direct route to the south.

He found a small spring at dusk where Goldy and he could drink. There was herbage for the sorrel, and he had food in his warsack.

The Ranger led Goldy a short way into the chaparral, picketed him, and retired to roll himself in his blanket under a small rock bluff. He had ridden a long distance since morning, and it did not take many minutes for him to fall asleep.

Hatfield had not been sleeping for long. He woke with a faint start. Overhead a billion stars gleamed in the milky sky, silvered by a half moon that seemed to rest on the tip of a darkly outlined mountain peak.

The Ranger did not move, but lay silently, staring up at the heavens. He knew no dream had disturbed him. But a feeling of danger gave him an innate, almost instinctive warning that he was threatened. He caught the faint rustle of the breeze in the dry bush, and a few thuds as Goldy stamped his hoofs on the ground. Such noises were natural and his ears were used to them.

Mystified, finally deciding some animal had strayed near him in the darkness, he shut his eyes and again slept.

A few minutes later he awoke once more, that same queer warning ticked in his brain. The shadows were deep about him; the thirty-foot high mescal plants looked like tortured giants in the night.

Instinctively, his hand went to the six-gun lying at his side. For a moment he tried to decide what was lurking in the underbrush. Mountain lions would not dare attack a man; he heard no warning such as a rattler might give.

Goldy sniffed and snorted. Without further warning Hatfield silently rose up. Cautiously, he hunted about him, but found nothing.

He shifted his camp a hundred yards to the east and went to sleep once more. A third time, minutes later, he was aroused.

"Who's that?" he demanded.

There was no reply save a faint wind rustle. Then he lay down and feigned sleep. After a quarter hour he heard a sound like a large snake slithering over a rock; to the untrained ear it would have been almost inaudible. He sent a shot into the dense bushes, and something scurried away full-speed through the brush.

The Ranger was not again disturbed.

In the grey dawn he rose, cooked coffee and bacon, squatting by his small fire. When the full light came he looked around the spots where he had slept.

The Lone Wolf was an expert trailer and tracker; he could read sign with the best scout, training and instinct greatly adding to his power. Sight, sound, hearing and touch, even smell, came to his aid. A mere scratch, the displacement of a natural object such as a stick or stone, would tell such a man a volume.

There was little to discover in the dry, pebbly earth. But he did find one sign — a broken twig, freshly cracked, by the weight of whatever had tried to creep up on him during the night.

When he went to saddle Goldy, there was another sign. In the sky to the west several distinct white puffs of smoke shot up. His grey-green eyes narrowed, he stared that way for moments — Indian smoke signals.

Jim Hatfield had been in many tight spots in his work as a Texas Ranger. When he had carried Lone Star Law into the Big Bend country, he had looked into the ugly, sneering face of a dirty death, a noose around his neck when he had been mistaken for a rustler by the aroused cowpunchers of the section. He had lived days on end with danger when he had smashed the big city crooks who sought to pirate the Alamita Basin oil lands. And he had fought for others and himself when trapped in a cinnabar mine, threatened by slow, torturesome death from mercury poisoning.

He did not doubt but that he had escaped by a hair during the night. If the men sending those smoke signals were Indians, it would explain their ability to come so close to him, nearly take him. Only his sixth sense had saved him.

Hatfield shrugged off his experience of the night before. Mounting Goldy he shoved on south. The taps of his stirrups brushed the thorny bushes, and lashed at the thick hide of his chaps protecting his legs from cactus and mesquite thorns. It was tough going at times and hard to ease Goldy through the winding openings of the wilderness trail. He watched for sign, bearing in mind that Gila Mike was hiding between his swooping depredations.

A small brook wound in a shallow ravine. Goldy splashed through, the Ranger's keen eye watching for quicksand. The golden horse paused to suck a drink. Hatfield noted the imprint of another hoof in the soft mud of the stream bank. It was an unshod hoof — possibly a wild horse come down to drink. But up the bank was a faint impression of a foot — a foot that had been encased in a moccasin.

" 'Twas an Indian, shore enough," he mused. "Tried to drygulch me."

As he climbed on toward the mountains, he kept looking back. At last noted several black specks winging eastward from the trail he had been following.

"Crows," he muttered.

They told him something moved in the thickets. It might be a natural enemy, coyote or weasel; then again, it might be a man following him.

He rude on south, intending to circle and catch his mysterious tracker, when he came to a favorable spot. The hills rose on either side, the trail following the way of least resistance.

After a time he swung through a rapidly narrowing gulch, which took him to the mouth of a shadowed, deeply-cut pass, with high rock walls. He could not see around the turn, and he pulled up, eyes seeking the ledges commanding the trail. The Ranger was thinking it was a perfect place for an ambush. He would hide Goldy, climb up and wait. Thus he would see who was following him.

Hatfield swung his foot from the right stirrup, his sombrero snapped on its strap, as though a swift hand had tried to slap it off. The dull thud of the bullet which had passed through the felt struck the rock at his right and spattered bits of granite on Goldy's flank.

He was in action as the rifle report crackled in the gulch.

CHAPTER V
HIDALGO'S REVENGE

Jim Hatfield leaped to the earth, dragging on Goldy's rein to jerk the sorrel out of range. A second slug tore close past them, then they were sheltered by an overhanging rock bluff.

The Ranger saw nobody above him when he peered out, but he heard a dislodged rock slide down in the confined pass. He leaped out and fired a shot at the steplike ledges on his left, hoping to draw his assailant into sight.

"Come out and fight," he roared.

No more bullets came at him. He ran toward the pass, looking for a way up, to get the man who had tried to shoot him

54

down. High up above him he could hear his assailant scrambling away.

Hatfield swung around a sharp turn, and the sight he saw brought him up short. The gap was blocked by masses of picked skeletons of men and animals. He had to climb over the jumbled mass. The heaps of bones had been bleached white by the hot sun after they had been savagely cleaned by coyotes and buzzards.

Whoever had been up there was on the run, ducking on a slant along the wooded mountain slope. Hatfield was unable to find a way up till he had traveled several hundreds yards and the pass widened out. Climbing to the summit, using handholds of jutting rocks and wiry bushes that found root in the scant dirt between the stones, he mounted higher and higher.

By the time he reached a point where he could survey the steep slope and the country to the south, the gunman was gone. Far below, Hatfield glimpsed a man wearing a steeple sombrero, low over the neck of a swift running horse.

When Hatfield returned to the canyon, he read the story of the massacre. Men had evidently lain hidden up on those ledges, caught the riders and their mules in a terrible gunfire and killed them all. Gaping bullet holes were visible in skulls and larger bones.

The Ranger worked his way to the lower level. He knew that whoever was behind him would not come up now, the shooting would warn him.

He walked Goldy through the choked pass, and, remounting, set out at a fast clip along the route taken by the sombreroed rider. The trail followed the path of necessity, keeping off cliffs and mountain sides as far as possible. He saw the tracks of the horse ahead, stones with unweathered sides, broken sticks, newly-smashed plants where the hoofs had struck.

Well on his way into the wild, deserted country Hatfield paused after nightfall. He picketed Goldy and hid himself in the rocks to sleep, alert even while he dozed.

Riding on, next day, he reached the Rio Grande. As far as he could see, the country ahead was deserted, mainly volcanic in origin. The man in the steeple hat had crossed into Mexico. The jurisdiction of the Texas Rangers ended at the Line, but Hatfield took the shooting at himself as a personal matter, and splashed Goldy on across the shallow, sandy river.

It was dusk when he came on the little

Mexican village, nestling in the hills. He walked the sorrel between the lines of adobe huts. One was larger than the rest, and the sound of guitars and many Mexican voices told the Ranger this was the cantina.

He dismounted and went to the door. Mexicans in high-peaked hats, clothes trimmed with ornaments, wearing serapes or other colorful garments, sat around imbibing tequila and wine.

Hatfield stepped inside, his tall Stetson top nearly touching the low ceiling.

His sudden appearance disconcerted the thirty men inside the place. They stared at the tall, wide-shouldered Ranger, whose cool eyes surveyed them.

A man in the rear, a handsome young Mexican with sideburns showing on the smooth flow of his brown cheeks, by far the best-dressed person in the cantina, suddenly leaped to his feet. His chair tipped back with a crash.

"*Cien mil diablos!* Kill him — kill the gringo!" he shrieked in Spanish.

He whipped out a pistol and fired a hurried shot which whirled close past Hatfield's head and buried itself in the adobe wall.

The cantina was at once in pandemonium. A gleaming knife hissed through the smoky air, slashed a piece from Hatfield's shirt arm and quivered with point buried in the panel behind. Guns came out as the Ranger jumped to the end of the short bar. The fusillade of the excited Mexicans tore the spot he had occupied an insant before.

The peons screeched in excitement, tossing knives and bullets at him. Fortunately the bar was of a wood thick enough to stop them. Hatfield did not wish to return the Mexicans' fire. Evidently, they were trying to kill him at the hidalgo's order; for the Don was as excited as the rest, crying for Hatfield's blood.

The Lone Wolf had his six-guns ready. The Mexican bartender had run around the other end of the bar and ducked for cover. Coolly the Ranger stayed down till the first spasm of fury was over. When his voice could be heard, he roared in Spanish:

"Stop it. I'm a friend!"

"Kill him — kill all gringos!" It was the young don who so thirsted for his blood.

But his refusal to return their fire gave the peons pause. The don shot at him till he emptied his six-shooter. As he started to reload, dark eyes flashing and face twisted, Hatfield ducked along the bar and vaulted over the top, landing close to the fiery Mexican. He snatched the six-gun from the slim hand, whirled the hidalgo around in front of him, handling him as easily as he might a child. The peons dared not shoot at him now, since they might hit their leader.

"Stop it," repeated Hatfield calmly, in the struggling man's ear. "I ain't goin' to hurt yuh, *amigo mio.* Yuh got things wrong. Yuh tried to drygulch me back there in that death gulch, but I ain't holdin' any hard feelin's. Keep still and let's talk 'bout this."

"Take your hands off me, Americano!" snarled the don. He had a hot, untameable spirit, proud Spanish blood flowing in his veins.

"Tell me why yuh're so on the prod," insisted Jim Hatfield, tightly holding him to prevent him from doing any more damage. "Whatever it is, it ain't my fault. Tell yore men to keep back, I don't want to hurt anybuddy."

The vaqueros and peons bunched a few yards off as Hatfield spoke to the ruffled don.

Hatfield's strong, forceful personality, and the deep resonance of his voice had calmed the men. Those who were not evil had nothing to fear from him. Men trusted the Ranger instinctively.

There was a mystery here Hatfield wished to solve. The don was torn with some kind of vengeance; but the Ranger did not want to use his gun to defend himself, for, the Lone Wolf never killed unless necessity demanded it. Though the Mexican had tried to drygulch him, he did not have the look of a Border gunman.

"Your hands off me, Senor," said the don but with not much insistence.

"Siddown and we'll talk it over. If yuh still wish to fight me when we're through, we'll take up the battle where we left off."

Still flushed with rage, slight figure shaking, the hidalgo stood stiffly as Hatfield calmly sat down. He faced the cantina, and his cool nerve plus his apparent disdain of death and refusal to hurt anyone, appealed to the spirit of the Mexicans. They made no attempt to rush him.

The don folded his arms on his breast, head high in pride. "It's no use," he said hotly. "I, Don Ramon Acosta, have made a vow to kill every gringo who sets foot in sight of me."

"Why?" The Ranger's face bore a puzzled look.

Don Ramon shrugged his slight shoulders. "Because of the murder of my brother Luis and fifty of his followers. Practically every person in my village here lost a relative and friends. You came through death canyon —

60

it bears enough evidence, does it not?

"I have waited there for weeks. You were lucky. Had you not moved as I fired, I would have added another to my list."

"But yuh don't know who wiped out yore brother?"

"No, senor. But I'll find out!"

Don Ramon, staring into the Ranger's grey-green eyes, knew that Hatfield was his master. He read the power of the man, sensed that he was a force for good.

"Stop shootin' Americans — leastways till yuh know who they are," ordered Hatfield. "If I ketch yuh at that agin, Don Ramon, I'll make mucho trouble for yuh. On the other hand, I mean to take the dogs who done that massacre on American soil, savvy?"

Don Ramon's brown eyes widened, and he looked long at the Ranger. "Senor, I believe you will do it," he replied at last. He raised his hand.

The bartender came out from cover, bringing them glasses and a bottle. The Ranger began to drink tequila with the man who a few short moments before had vowed to take his life.

Then Hatfield learned Don Ramon's story. Don Luis, the hidalgo's elder brother and chief of the small village nestling in the hills, had started north with a pack-train laden down with silver and many goods made by the peon artisans. These peons were the pride of the Acosta family. They made beautiful, rare copies of the old Aztec pottery and did fine carvings, the skill of which had been handed down for generations.

"The death of so many of our people, the robbery of our goods, has almost ruined our village," Don Ramon said. "We needed the money my brother would have brought back, to pay taxes and other things. We may lose our lands.

"If you wish to spend the night at my hacienda on the hill near here, I will be glad to show you some of the things my people make. I am sure you will believe me when I say their murder is a great loss."

Hatfield nodded. He slept that night in a soft bed, the guest of Don Ramon Acosta. In the morning, he and the don made a tour of the village, going from hut to hut seeing the work the peons had done.

Heading northward again in the dawn, Hatfield swung to the west after crossing the river, following another route from the one traveled. He wished to get a general idea of the whole territory.

Miles past the Rio Grande, on American soil, he saw smoke in the distance. The country was vast, breathtaking in its sweep. The bald top of a high mountain peak dominated the land. He began to cross old lava, black and broken, once a molten river of fire.

The smoke came from a small settlement. The location bothered Hatfield; it was set in a gaplike valley between the bald top mountain, which, by the traces of the lava, evidently had once been in eruption, and another peak on the east.

Goldy was covered with burrs, mane tangled with thorns, sorrel body damp with sweat as the Ranger walked him down the narrow valley, crossed a silver brook and headed for the town.

It consisted of a dozen new and quickly thrown together brush and adobe-brick shacks. Only one building was of any size, and that was the saloon, marked with a pair of longhorns painted silver.

"Never heard tell of this place," he murmured. "Funny Davis didn't mention it."

Pack mules and saddle horses stood around, and men lounged in the shade. Far up on Bald Top, the western mountain, specks of men showed as they moved.

The travel-stained Ranger rode to the rear

of the Silver Steer and dismounted stiffly. A small man stepped from the shade and stared at him.

"Give him a feed and rub down, best yuh got."

Spurs clanking, the long-legged Ranger strode around the side of the saloon and up the three steps to the low porch. There were men in the place, lounging at rough-cut tables with drinks or playing cards. The odor of fresh wood was in the air, bright, new sawdust on the floor. A bartender ambled up, looked Hatfield over, nodded. He seemed very curious.

"Howdy," he said flatly. "Warm, ain't it, mister? Come far?"

Hatfield let his cool eyes travel to the broad face. There was a bulge under the white apron, showing the barkeeper was armed for trouble.

"I'll have whiskey," Hatfield replied.

The bartender flushed and hurried to set out the liquor.

Hatfield felt that he was being covertly watched by the men in the saloon. He shifted a little, as though by chance, so he could cover his back.

A scrawny man with a marshal's five-pointed star pinned to his flapping vest, handlebar mustache working on a pockmarked face, hustled into the saloon. The marshal had come on a run, the Ranger could tell that from the way he was panting. Someone must have warned him there was a strange waddy in the place.

"Howdy," said the marshal. "Kin I help yuh, mister?"

"Why, no," drawled the Ranger, taking a sip of his drink. "Don't know as I need any help." It was strange how excited everybody got on account of a person drawing up for a rest to wet his whistle.

The marshal tried again. "My name's Crole, mister. I got charge of law and order in Corellez —"

"Good," replied Hatfield.

"Drinks 're on me." Crole gave up trying to discover the identity of the tall stranger.

The sun rode like a huge red ball on the rugged, bare-topped mountain; there were trees and brush like a spread of whiskers around the widening shoulders and base of the peak. Through the open door, Hatfield looked and saw a young woman who stood gazing up the winding path that led to the summit of Bald Top. It was Edith Voorhees.

"So this is where they headed to!" mused Hatfield. There was some secret up there on the dead volcano.

Hans Voorhees, Edith's stout father, wearing khaki breeches and high laced boots, a battered felt hat, a walking stick in hand, appeared on the path. With him was a tall, strange looking man with a face so chalky that it was noticeable even at that distance. Behind them came Bert Selkirk, and the wizened professor. A number of hombres dressed like prospectors brought up the end of the procession. Selkirk left the group and joined Edith and they strolled off together.

Vance was on the stout Voorhees' other flank, speaking to him with evident enthusiasm. They all came to the Silver Steer. Crole left Hatfield, stepped over and whispered to the pale-faced fellow. A crease deepened in the pallid brow, he excused himself from the table where he had led Voorhees, and came to Hatfield at the bar.

The armed men in the place stiffened, the air grew tense. The Ranger was ready for anything.

"Stranger," said the pale-faced man, a sharp edge to his voice, "we can't help wonderin' what you're doing down here."

"Why," replied Hatfield softly, "didn't know I had to give excuses to dampen my throat?"

The pasty face did not change, though the brows drew together. "This," he announced, "is my camp, private. It's named Corellez, after me."

"Yuh got quite a set-up, Corellez. Yore town shore growed like a mushroom. I didn't hear tell of it in Brewster."

Corellez cleared his throat. His eyes were fixed on the big Ranger, whose power was readable in every line of the relaxed, supple body. His non-descript clothes did not fool the man; there was authority of some sort.

"We keep our mouths shut for a good reason. Though I wonder if my activities bring you down here?"

Hatfield shrugged. "Told yuh I jest stopped in fer a drink." To himself he mused, "Don't care too much 'bout this Corellez. Reminds me of a talkin' ghost, he's right clammy. Don't seem to wish to force a scrap but don't care for my company."

"Marshal Crole'll be glad to give you a hand at anything, in case you're looking for someone," Corellez added.

"Much obliged." Hatfield considered the whole set-up mysterious. It might be a mine strike of some sort; these men would not want the news to leak outside as yet. Corellez, mentioning the town marshal he had appointed, told the Ranger that they suspected him of being a law officer. But they did not know he was a Texas Ranger; they probably believed him to be a special deputy appointed by Marshal Davis of Brewster, and that suited Hatfield.

The faces of some in the Silver Steer were hard, the sort Hatfield often had to do with professionally. They looked like gunmen and riffraff, but that kind usually drifts in to a mining town, in fact, always may be found in the small settlements of the southwest country.

So far everyone was well-behaved. But the air of constraint did not loosen. Rather, it tightened as Corellez, plainly out of patience with the big man's uncommunicativeness, swung with a scowl on his pale face returned to his party.

Meditatively turning his glass in his long fingers, the Lone Wolf noted that George Vance questioned Corellez, and that the latter shrugged, gave some reply to which Voorhees and Vance listened carefully. The eccentric millionaire, fat belly pushed against the edge of the rough slab table, watched Hatfield with open suspicion, face red, deep wrinkles between his thick-glassed, near-sighted eyes.

Darkness dropped over the small town of Corellez. A wind rustled in the dry herbage of the mountains; there had been no rain for many weeks. The odor of wild flowers and sagebrush mingled with the familiar smell of whiskey and freshness of newly-cut sawdust.

More men had come into the Silver Steer; their clothing was stained with dirt, and they looked rather like miners who had been at work. The large square room grew crowded. Card games went on here and there, but the place was unusually quiet.

There was a table down the room where food was sold. The Ranger made his way to it through the groups of men, who did not speak to him, simply eyed him.

"They shore don't have out welcome sign," he mused.

A couple of men got up from a faro game on the side of the large room. They strolled to the bar and landed close to Hatfield.

Alert, although seemingly uninterested in what went on about him, Hatfield kept an eye on them; they seemed to have some definite purpose in view. Sheriff Crole sauntered off, turning his back to the bar.

Both hombres were flinty of face, and wore their guns high, with reversed butts, as though very familiar with them. Jim Hatfield knew the type; they were the sort who would do anything for pay.

The taller was a wolfish fellow in a black Stetson, who held his chin out and up. He was now almost touching Hatfield's elbow, and he stared insolently into the Ranger's calm visage.

"Say, feller," he growled, "didn't I meet up with yuh last year over El Paso way?" His speech was a little thick; he had been drinking heavily.

"They're shore soundin' me out," thought Hatfield. Aloud, he politely replied, "Why, it's possible."

The Lone Wolf lapsed into a deep silence. He was thinking of Gila Mike Turner, the giant bandit, who, he was sure, knew about the death of Ranger Martin.

This secret camp, the obvious uneasiness with which they looked on the coming of a stranger, aroused his official curiosity. Good beef cattle had been disappearing into the south; what more probable than that it was being used here in Corellez? Such a gang would need plenty of meat.

Voorhees, Vance, and others who had been in the pack train he had passed, had seen him heading south. Also, they had been aware of his play in Brewster, when he had arrested the two who had wounded Professor Jackson.

Hatfield's refusal to grow talkative irritated the man in the black hat as much as it had the town boss, Corellez. And the former was a man of action.

"Polecats allus rides alone," he remarked loudly to his comrade.

The Ranger's jaw tightened. They were trying to draw him, it was plain. To bite now would only please them so he pretended not to have heard the insult. But the man in the black Stetson was determined on making trouble. He lurched, fell heavily against Hatfield.

"Say, polecat," he snarled, "watch out who yuh're bumpin'!"

"Now look," Hatfield told him levelly, "there's plenty room at the other end of the bar. I ain't aimin' to be mixin' with yuh."

The Ranger's effort to keep the peace amused the pair mightily. They laughed till the tears rolled from their eyes.

"Why, he's got a yella streak!" the second man shouted. "He looks right salty but when he comes to the turn danged if he don't go right off the edge!"

The one in the black hat kept pushing in. "Say, we got a law in this town that a man has to check his hawglegs with the barkeep, young feller. Push yores over the bar, pronto

— or mebbe yuh don't consider yoreself a man."

Marshal Crole was over on the other side of the room; many eyes watched the play, but no one said anything.

"I'm holdin' on to my guns," replied Hatfield. This game was a familiar one. They were going to force him to start a scrap and then end it their own way, two to one.

Emboldened by the Ranger's refusal to bristle up, the hombre in the black hat reached out a dirty paw to snatch Hatfield's pistol. The Lone Wolf caught the wiry wrist in a grip of steel.

"Better go on down to the other end of the bar," he drawled easily. "This is yore last warnin'."

A look of amazement, into which crept fear as the gunman felt the mighty grip of the Ranger, flashed in the dark eyes.

"Leggo," he snarled. "Leggo, damn yuh —"

His mate, protected by the other's body, had put a hand to his chin as though to scratch it. He dropped that hand limply and then it flashed up in a swift draw.

Hatfield whirled the man he held and violently threw him against the gunman, knocked him backward. The man in the black hat lost his head and went for his smooth-handled Colt .45. Without a waste motion, Hatfield grabbed it as it cleared leather, twisted it out of his grip, reversed it and covered the two.

"Yuh told me yoreself the rule is to check guns with the bartender, boys so go to it." The voice was easy, but there was more than a kind of steel in it.

The other, having seen what the big man with the cold grey-green eyes did to his friend, made no further attempt to shoot. He quickly dropped his drawn revolver on the top of the bar. Then Hatfield placed the tall man's Colt beside it.

"Keep these for the boys till they sober up," he said loudly to the bartender.

"Damn yuh," growled the man in the black sombrero. "Yuh'll be sorry fer this. Me'n yuh might meet some dark and lonely night, savvy?"

Marshal Crole came bustling up. "Here, what's goin' on?" he demanded. "What's the idea of the gunplay, mister?" He frowned angrily at Hatfield as though blaming him for the whole thing.

Hatfield turned his back to the bar, elbows draped on the edge. From the corner of his eye he saw a man enter the Silver Steer, up at the front door. He was huge of body, tall as the Ranger and much heavier through the torso. Over his left eye, which was half-closed by the puckering of the flesh, showed plainly a scar, a livid cross in the dark tan of his skin.

The Ranger had listened carefully to the descriptions of Gila Mike Turner, and had actually glimpsed the bandit during the raid on Brewster jail when they had attempted to rescue the pair who had shot up Professor Jackson. He had no doubt that the man he was seeking was now in the same room with him.

His cold eyes fixed on the huge killer. As he started to go up to the front of the Silver Steer, to seize Turner, Marshal Crole blocked him.

"Looka here, I was speakin' to yuh, mister," Crole insisted. "We don't allow gun-plays in our town. I'm appointed to keep order and I'm doin' it. Hand over yore guns if yuh wish to stay."

His loud voice drew the attention of Gila Mike. The bandit stood just inside the doorway, looking over the gathering. He had had a fair sight of Hatfield in the jail, and he immediately recognized the Ranger.

Crole noticed the Ranger's sudden interest. He glanced back over his shoulder and saw Gila Mike.

Crole dived for his six-gun and blocked

Hatfield as the latter started at Turner. The town marshal sent a shot that whirled over Gila Mike's sombrero.

With a snarl the giant outlaw leaped back outside. As he moved he made a draw that was like the flash of lightning in its speed. Then, putting a couple of bullets into the ceiling, he jumped out of sight.

Hatfield threw Crole out of his way, lunging for the bat-wings. As he moved, the man in the black Stetson snatched up his pistol from the bar, and swung on the Ranger, lips twisted in a snarl of rage.

CHAPTER VI
NIGHT FIGHT

As Hatfield threw a quick slug after the vanished Turner, it was the man in the black hat who stopped the bullet. He had leaped around Crole in order to shoot the Ranger, and had jumped into the line of fire. A sharp crack sounded as the heavy bullet smashed his hip bone and he crashed to the sawdust knotted with pain.

Hatfield rushed to the door and was outside. He landed on the warm, dry dirt of the road, feet spread wide, Colt rising. Crole hurtled from the saloon, gun ready.

Hoofbeats sounded up the road. The dark

figure of a horseman, spurring away from the Silver Steer, bent low over his mount's neck, appeared for a moment.

"Halt!" roared the Ranger, starting forward.

A shot whistled back at him, despatched by the bandit on the great horse.

"Hey, waddy. Careful with them bullets!" cried Marshal Crole.

"I want that hombre," snapped Hatfield, shoving Crole out of the way.

But Gila Mike already invisible in the darkness, pounded past the shacks. Dust rose into the air, clouding the Ranger's vision.

There were plenty of saddled ponies at the Silver Steer hitch-racks. The Lone Wolf did not hesitate to borrow one. He snatched the reins of a big, raw-boned black, leaped into the saddle and spurred on Gila Mike Turner's trail.

Gila Mike had got off to a fast start. The Ranger stuck spurs into the black, and was off into the night. The dark shapes of mesquite bushes, like tortuous giants, loomed black on either side as he brushed past. To his left the bald-top mountain was an ominous, inky mass as he galloped north. The other hills, on the east, hemmed in the narrow gap.

A short distance north of Corellez, Hatfield was close enough to see Gila Mike turn off to the right, giving the quirt and spurs to his mount. In the thick bush, there was the glow of a campfire, a reddish blotch in the darkness. He swung the black's champing head that way, hotly intent on the chase.

Branches slapped at his face as he rode the faint trail to the fire. Coming up he saw beyond, touched by the flickering light of the wood flames, the outline of a rough brush and pole corral, and the dark shapes of steers inside it.

In the light of the smoky fire, he was suddenly aware of mounted men who spurred in on him from the flanks. A burst of gunfire sent slugs through his clothing; one bullet burned along his leg, shocking him with such violence that it sent him half off the black. Then, an instant later the great horse shrieked, leaping high into the air, ruining the Ranger's aim as he sought to return the hot attack.

Hatfield, leg drawn up with the pain, managed to disengage his other boot from the stirrup as the twelve-hundred pound black crashed with a terrific jolt to the ground. The Ranger was flung sideward, but he kept on rolling as the men bunched to finish him with their six-guns, slugs drilling the dirt.

The sharp end of a big boulder jabbed into Hatfield's back as he ended up against it, the violence of his own roll knocking out his wind. He straightened out his lithe, powerful body, just as a bullet smacked the flinty rock and spattered his face with fragments.

The Ranger whirled and the six-gun he kept gripped in his hand flared reddish-yellow at the horsemen almost upon him. Their excited ponies helped to spoil accurate aim, giving him the moment he needed to recover. The horse of the man in front reared and swerved at the explosion so close in his eyes. The animal went leaping past the crouched Ranger, the rider forced to fight the tossing, snorting head.

As the other four drove at him, the Lone Wolf flipped behind the jagged boulder and knocked one of his enemies out of the saddle.

The fusillade from their guns smacked the rock and tore the bush and dirt behind him. But he had the advantage of position, since they could not see him against the black background while they were framed in the firelight. Gila Mike Turner was roaring furiously at his men, urging them on.

"Git him outa there — tear him to pieces,"

bawled Turner. "That's the polecat who fought us in Brewster!"

Jim Hatfield's steady eyes glowed as he held them, head level with the top of his shielding rock. Slowly, ignoring the whistling bullets, he took aim at Turner. But another outlaw cut across as Hatfield released his hammer, taking the slug in the shoulder. His cries of pain sobered the others; they jerked hard on their reins, horses dancing back and away, out of the light.

Gila Mike pushed ahead of them; they left a man there on the ground, lying as he had fallen after the Ranger's lead had hit. The big black horse was stiffening nearby.

In the corral the cattle bellowed in fear, hoofs stamping. The light corral sides creaked as they strained under the impact of the maddened steers.

Out of the darkness the bandits still shot at Hatfield. He took aim at the flashes, making each shot carefully.

Then, in the stony bush behind him, he heard someone moving. The others kept shooting and yelling. A man had been sent to creep around and get the Ranger from the back, while his pals occupied him from the other side. But the brush was too thick to push through without making any sounds.

Only two were out there before him, mounted. They were toward the rough trail off which he had swung. The rock protected him from their slugs, which came with regularity. The nasty whine of the big bullets, the heavy explosions, filled his ears with din, but now and then he caught a faint rustle from the one who was creeping up behind him.

"Tryin' to keep me busy while their pal gits me in the spine," he growled.

A thick, gnarled mesquite bush, with blossoms like ghost stars in the darkness of the night, was close behind him. His keen ears were wide, to follow the movements of the gunman slowly crawling closer and closer.

The steady booming of the guns was annoying, for it prevented him from telling the exact position of the oncoming man. The noises behind him suddenly ceased. Hatfield rolled to one side, and a pistol flashed, boomed almost in his ear, the slug striking the rear face of the jagged boulder.

Across his body he fired once, twice, through the mesquite. No doubt the drygulcher was able to see him, since the Ranger was toward the fire. From back of the bush a man gave a loud shriek that cut off suddenly short in a choked gurgle.

"Hey, Sam!" Gila Mike's great voice

roared. "Yuh git him?"

Sam did not reply. He lay there, drilled through the lungs, on the other side of the mesquite clump.

The mighty Lone Wolf shoved fresh shells into his hot pistols. One in hand, the second holstered, he began to creep along the line of brush that framed the clearing, lips a taut line. If he could get close enough to Gila Mike.

The steers were bellowing, adding to the uproar. Gila Mike was still shooting at the big rock. The giant outlaw believed Hatfield to be there.

There was a sudden groaning crash of overstrained wood, as the whole side of the corral gave way under the pushing weight of forty or fifty animals. The released beasts, raising their tails and putting down their horned heads, snorted and stampeded out, high, wide and handsome.

They ran, dark shapes in the fire's glow, across the Ranger's vision, splitting into bunches and charging the thorny brush. A couple of the animals nearly trampled on the Ranger. He put a bullet into the closest, and the steer fell head over heels, lay still.

"Look out, Jess," shouted Gila Mike.

The outlaws swung, retreating before the maddened cows, every one a prime head of beef in full power. The Ranger leaped backward as they sent a final blind, furious volley of lead back at him. He wished to have a look at the man who had crept up on him.

He found the body, stretched with face buried in the sandy earth, behind the mesquite bush. He quickly struck a match, rolling the hombre over. It was, he saw, a hard, brutal face, teeth clenched in death, stain of blood on the lips. Plainly one of Gila Mike's killers.

He cut through the brush, weaving toward the trail, gun ready in hand. His wounded leg burned and he felt the sticky warm blood oozing down his thigh.

All bandit horses had run off in the little stampede. The Ranger, choked, half-blinded by the dust raised, pushed out to the open way. Gila Mike was gone, galloping northward, hell-for-leather.

Mounted men came from the south, saw the tall, dark form of the Lone Wolf there. One of them shouted and fired a shot that passed over Hatfield's head, whipping the bush like a cracking cowhide.

CHAPTER VII
THE LEAD-OFF

The Ranger swung to face them, pistol leveled, cold eyes narrowed.

"Who's that?" a gruff voice demanded. But there was no rush to approach Hatfield. They came slowly, almost diffidently.

It was Marshal Crole, and the pallid-faced Corellez rode behind the marshal, a couple of other men flanking the town boss. George Vance brought up the rear of the procession, too, looking at the tall Ranger. They drew rein, waiting as the Lone Wolf stared at the marshal.

"Okay, Marshal, the scrap's over," drawled Hatfield.

He swung and stalked back to the clearing in the bush. Some dry wood lay near the fire and he tossed on several big limbs, fanning up the blaze with his Stetson. He knelt by the steer he had shot, and on the shoulder there was the foot-high brand, ME Connected. So this was where Milton English's cows had been brought!

"It was Gila Mike kilt that line rider, Buck Stamford, then," he concluded.

Crole and the others came toward him almost gingerly. "Say, hold yore fire now, mister," the marshal growled. They had dismounted near the fire.

"No hard feelin's, are there, mister?" The Ranger didn't miss the slight quaver in Crole's tone.

Plainly the Ranger's ability to protect himself had over-awed the officer.

Corellez's strange face was even more bizarre in the ruby glow of the fire. He looked like a death's head as he faced Hatfield.

"See here, fella," he snapped. "That's my black horse you took. Look at him. He ain't much good for anything now." He pointed to the dead animal. "Some places they don't approve of hombres who take horses that don't belong to 'em. In fact they call 'em —"

"Let's fergit what they call em," broke in the Ranger softly. There was some justice to the complaint of the boss. "I'm willin' to pay for yore horse."

Marshal Crole cleared his throat. "Say, — if we knowed yuh wanted Gila Mike so all-fired bad and had come all the way down here after him, things would've bin diff'rent. We ain't outlaws."

"Of course not," declared Corellez.

The Lone Wolf did not offer any explanations. He allowed them to stew in their own juice. He pointed to the dead steer.

84

"The beef yuh meant to eat," he remarked succinctly, "has got a trademark."

Vance stepped forward, bent over and examined the brand. "ME," he read. "Who's that?"

"ME Connected," corrected Crole. "Rustled, by gravy!"

"What?" cried Corellez hotly. "Where's that hombre I gave that beef contract to?"

"Must've had a connection with Gila Mike," Crole said. "Turner ain't in the habit of comin' open-like into our town," he went on, to Hatfield. "I wouldn't allow it, no sir! He's a no-good bandit. They bin skinnin' them cows in the bush and deliverin' us beef ready to cook. It shore fooled us."

Hatfield cleared his throat. "I wonder," he thought to himself, "how much yuh think yuh're foolin' me, Marshal?" Aloud he asked, "How much for the horse, Corellez?"

"Oh, you can't make him pay for that!" George Vance cried. "Why, he's an officer, chasing rustlers, Mr. Corellez. I'll pay for that animal myself first."

"Forget it," Corellez ordered. "Forget the horse. I've got plenty more, friend —What'd yuh say your name is?"

"I didn't, but call me James."

"All right — James. Yuh sure don't waste

85

breath talking, do yuh? But you're okay in Corellez, young fella." The town boss's tone was hearty. He raised a hand as though to slap the big man on the back, but catching those cold, level eyes, thought better of it and changed the motion to scratch his ear instead.

"We want to help you and we will," he declared. "All we want is to be undisturbed, sir, we've no wish to have any trouble with the law."

"I think," Vance said, in his cultivated tone, "you ought to tell him, Corellez. After all, he must wonder what all this secrecy is about."

Hatfield looked at the man with the dude's mustache. He had an air of vitality about him, suggesting intelligence and power.

"Maybe so," agreed Corellez. To Hatfield he said, "We made a strike on Bald Top Mountain, you see, a treasure strike we've kept secret, for we don't want the whole world trooping down here as yet.

"Naturally, busy as we've been, we haven't checked up on our source of supplies and evidently this Gila Mike's been cleaning up at both ends, stealing cattle to sell us. He's kept behind one of his men, we didn't know we were dealing with him. I've heard a rumor or two since I came down here, that

Turner has a hideout east of here. You know about that, Crole?"

"Oh, yeah, yeah," Crole declared firmly. "I ain't never chased him myself, because he's pretty careful when he's in Corellez."

"You know the approximate location of Turner's den, Crole," went on Corellez. "In the morning, Marshal, you can start this officer on his way.

"Glad to do that," Crole agreed.

"Much obliged," drawled Hatfield.

The Ranger's warm guns had been slipped back into the supple, oiled holsters. Having seen all there was to see at the rustlers' corral, Hatfield borrowed a horse which had belonged to one of the dead bandits. Mounting, Hatfield trotted back with Corellez, Vance and the marshal to the town.

Had Corellez, he wondered, glancing at the ghastly face, ordered his minions to draw him into a scrap at the saloon to get rid of him? But Hatfield had proved too salty for them. They had concluded he had been sent from Brewster, to catch Gila Mike.

Now Crole and Corellez were mighty interested in his movements, wished to get him out of the way. Well, he'd go with Crole in the morning.

Gila Mike had strolled into that Silver

Steer saloon as though he owned the place. Turner might have considered himself safe, unknown down there. But the Lone Wolf smelled a mangy odor, concluded that if he was sent one way, it was to keep him from looking the other. They wanted to get rid of him and keep themselves clean with the law in Brewster. Why, he didn't know. But he would find out.

Of course, if they had a gold strike up on the hill, it might explain their desire to keep things quiet. They wouldn't want a stampede till everything was settled, claims proved and filed.

The saloon was about empty when they looked in. Yellow lights showed in several of the rough shacks.

"Crole'll find you a bunk tonight," said Corellez hospitably.

"Thanks, but I ain't bed-slept so long I'd jest toss all night."

The Lone Wolf saddled up Goldy and rode into the deep bush a mile away from town. He made camp carefully and slept with both ears and one eye open.

The morning broke cloudless. Greyness was still in the sky when the Ranger woke, but the air was keen with dawn. Over the valley gap the eastern mountain cast a great dark shadow, damp with clinging mist, but on mighty Bald Top the sun tipped the reddish-black dirt with a cap of glorious red.

Hatfield saddled up and rode into Corellez. Breakfast was in order, he smelled frying bacon and coffee boiling. There were armed men around but none bothered the big Ranger. Crole hustled to greet him from the Silver Steer.

"Come on, fella. While I'm saddlin' up, the cook'll give yuh a handout."

Voorhees, stretching and yawning, came out from a shack. George Vance and the wizened little Dr. Green stepped out of another hut. Young Bert Selkirk smiled at the fair sky. They all stared up at Bald Top Mountain. Hatfield went to the kitchen where he filled up on cakes and coffee. Crole was waiting for him when he finished.

Crole and the Ranger, mounting, rode out of Corellez and turned south through trackless country. They came to a black lava stream where, ages before, that bald-headed mountain had blown its cone off and spewed forth millions of tons of molten rock. The rock had flowed the way of least resistance, widening here, narrowing there, seeking lower levels, till it had cooled and petrified.

That had been long ago and the chaparral had grown around the edges. In and out of the bush the marshal led the Ranger, letting the ponies pick a route, avoiding rougher iron-hard spots.

Crole turned at an eastward angle and they began to cross the southern side of the less distinctive mountain which flanked the valley on the east. The heavy breathing of the horses, the creak of leather, and the roll of a stone now and then under a hoof, broke the quiet of the lovely, majestic wilderness. As they traveled the coolness and shade evaporated in the rays of the warm sun.

Crossing a wide open space of rocks, a whining thing like an invisibly swift insect tore over their heads, hit with a dull spat behind their backs.

"That was a bullet, fella!" gasped Crole. "C'mon, let's make for cover!"

"Rifle, and long distance, a mile anyways," said Hatfield calmly.

"They must've spotted us, mister," Crole said shakily.

They crossed to the other side of the mountain. Crole sat his saddle, pointed long arm toward a bluish hill way off to the southeast.

"See them two straight buttes, pard? Keep yore hoss's haid between 'em. Yuh'll find a way through and when yuh're halfway down the slope on the other side of 'em, keep a sharp eye for a limestone ledge grown with scrub pine. They say Gila Mike's cave is there. He figgers no one kin git at him, and mebbe he's right. Watch yore ridin'."

"Much obliged," drawled the Lone Wolf.

Crole sat there, watching him ride off. Whoever had sent that rifle bullet, almost spent when it reached the Ranger, was not in sight. The Ranger looked back once and Crole raised his arm in farewell. There was a relieved expression on the marshal's scarred, mustached face.

Hatfield headed as directed. When he came into a patch of timber that hid him entirely, he swung and, looking back, saw that Crole was on his way home. The Ranger let the big sorrel pick a way slowly over the rough pine-covered slope.

Sure that Crole had returned to Corellez, believing the troublesome Hatfield gone for at least two or three days, the Lone Wolf stopped Goldy. He dismounted and crept up on a high rock bluff, from which he could look down and see Crole plodding back toward Bald Top.

He waited a while, hand on Goldy's muzzle. When Crole had a good start, the Ranger remounted and headed directly south. He was careful to seek patches of cover, and not allow the sun to strike any exposed metal of his accoutrements; such a flash may be seen many miles.

"Well, Goldy," he murmured, "we'll shore find out what it is Corellez is so all-fired anxious to hide. And I think we'll ketch Gila Mike a lot nearer than our friend Crole claims. Imagine tryin' to stampede us with that long-distance rifle shootin'!"

Chapter VIII
The Apaches

Bert Selkirk was rather weary from the long day spent on Bald Top. He was also very confused and puzzled. The enthusiasm of Professor Cassius Green, the famous expert, and of George Vance, who knew a great deal about the ancient Aztec treasure, had communicated itself to him and he had grown excited.

Hans Voorhees, with his fat stomach and near-sighted eyes, had had a difficult climb up to the hidden crater forming the head of Bald Top Mountain. Mules could wind fairly close to the summit but then it was necessary to go on foot over the rocks of the rim.

"I wish Dr. Jackson was here. He'd know," Selkirk said aloud.

They had not returned to Corellez till

after dark. Voorhees was closeted with Corellez, boss of the little town, discoverer and owner of the treasure.

It had been a great shock to Selkirk when Dr. Jackson had not been able to come to Corellez. He was the greatest authority on Aztec art in the United States, and his judgment would have been final. He had been wounded by a drunken cowboy during the saloon brawl in Brewster. Jackson had told Selkirk to go on and help Voorhees, who had asked the doctor's assistance in determining the value of the Corellez find.

The few samples displayed before they had come to Corellez had been authentic, valuable. There was an ancient sacrificial knife with an obsidian blade, and intricately carved handle encrusted with emeralds portraying Huitzilpochtl, Aztec War God. Jackson had declared it marvelous, a perfect example of the Aztec work.

He had also seen a beautiful carved bowl set with mosaic — this he knew to be ancient Aztec. The gorgeous colors were still effective. Vance had promised more startling primitive Mexican work with jade, agate, topaz, quartz, amethyst, sapphire and other precious stones. He also said there were pieces of their minute carvings in obsidian, volcanic glass, most remarkable of all their art.

The size of the deposits in the treasure cave had overwhelmed Selkirk. He had listened as Vance and Dr. Green exclaimed over one after another of the many objects Corellez and his aides exhibited in the dim light of the torches that illuminated the great caverns.

And Hans Voorhees' pale eyes gleamed with excitement behind the thick lenses of his glasses. Such objects might be sold at a tremendous profit. He would make another fortune at such a deal.

Bert Selkirk was a conscientious young man. He had been, for three years, working with Professor Jackson, and he was the latter's most brilliant pupil.

Pencil in hand, Selkirk had been trying to write a careful description of the wonders he had seen that day. He knew that Jackson would be eager to hear about it all.

The beads of sweat stood out on his clean, bronzed forehead. He had, he found, done nothing but repeat what he had heard others say. He had nodded when Voorhees asked his opinion, and agreed that he was sure the treasures were priceless. So had Cassius Green, and Vance. Green was second only to the fearless, powerful Jackson in knowledge and reputation, though he had none of Jackson's forceful personality. He was a dust-dry storehouse of knowledge, mentally existing back in the ages when Montezuma ruled the rugged mountains of Mexico and Cortez had not yet dared the impossible with his handful of Conquistadores.

The story of the treasure was very plausible. It was a known fact that many of the Aztec hiding-places for valuables remained undiscovered; every now and then a new one was unearthed. Emperor Montezuma and his people, fallen upon by the rapacious Spaniards, had desperately attempted to save some of their wealth by sending it to secret caves of the mountain fastnesses.

Runners had carried precious stones and metal into the hills. They were remarkable for their endurance and speed, could easily have come as far north as what now was southern Texas, climbed Bald Top, and placed the treasure in the volcanic caves. Their gods, they believed, inhabited volcanos, so they would favor such a spot and take care of the treasures.

"I've put every cent I had into unearthing these treasures," Corellez had said. "I need money and I'm willing to sell out." He had

had to pay the laborers who had cleaned out the débris of centuries because there had been small quakes which had closed some of the cave recesses.

The sweat still stood on Selkirk's brow. He had given Voorhees a recommendation to buy. The eccentric Dutchman was the father of the girl he loved. What if he had gone off half-cocked, and overestimated the value of that stuff? What would Edith think of him?

The price asked by Corellez was huge, one hundred and fifty thousand dollars. If the treasure was as good as it looked, it was cheap at the price, Voorhees could double his money by sales to museums and collectors. Voorhees himself was a rich man, a collector, but he was no expert in the sense that Jackson and Green were.

"Golden crowns — Aztec mosaic — codices and idols — strange carvings and statuettes. Tonatiah, the Sun-Chief, on whose altars unnumbered palpitating human hearts had been strewn. Xipe, the Flayed One, in obsidian with eyes of diamonds. The Plumed Serpent, and porphyry blocks; pottery figures and incense burners. Red, black, orange, ceramic ware of rainbow hue.

"Turquoise beads; a warrior shield, pieces

forming an elaborate design, set with pre-cious and semi-precious stones. Strange al-ligatorlike beasts in gold; arrows, metal birds. The doubleheaded snake —"

He rose determinedly, having come to his decision. He must have a look again, him-self, unswayed by the judgment of the oth-ers. He must make sure. Even now, Voorhees might be agreeing to invest a fortune in the enterprise.

He took a filled oil lantern and matches, then stuck a few biscuits in his pockets. There was a little spring up there from which he could drink. Then he put out his candle lamp and stepped into the cool night. There was noise coming from the lighted saloon. But Selkirk swung away in the shadows, heading for Bald Top and the caves of the Aztecs.

He caught a mule in a corral at the base of the mountain, cinched an old saddle on the sure-footed animal's back. Mounting, he pushed up Bald Top.

It was late when he finally arrived in the crater. There were spots where the lava deposit afforded no foothold for plants, but in others dirt had blown and sifted in the scrub brush grew. He knew the way, and a powdered dome of stars, with the quarter moon glowing in the sky, helped him on the stony path to the cave. A cool wind whined over the crater edges.

Breath coming fast, legs aching from the hard climb, Selkirk paused at a flat rock, rested the lantern on it, and struck a match. The flame flickered as he touched the burning stick to the blackened wick; he closed the glass, and letting the light come up, stepped into the entrance of the volcanic cave.

Inside were tarpaulins spread on the stony floor. On these rested some of the Aztec treasures. He knelt down, and began to inspect them closely by the light of his lantern. His breath sucked swiftly in and out of his lips.

He had been inside for about twenty minutes when a dark, half-naked figure appeared silently in the mouth of the cave and looked in at Selkirk. Immersed in his study of a decorated bowl, the young man did not see the man behind him. He was turning the bowl slowly in the light, a furrow between his handsome eyes.

He nearly jumped out of his skin, and the bowl flew out of his hands, broke in three pieces on the stone floor as the intruder without speaking touched him on the shoulder.

"Why — why — what are you doing here!" gasped Selkirk.

The man who had come upon him so stealthily wore an old pair of pants, his splay feet were bare. His legs were tremendously developed, and while he was not tall he gave an impression of great strength and endurance.

The straight black hair, cut roughly at the ears, was bound by a rattlesnake skin band. The eyes glowed like green-black coals; the nose was curved, the lips a straight blue line. There was no expression in the face save that sombre, dead impression caused by the immobility of the chiseled features. At his side he wore in a sheath a foot-long knife, its edge sharp as a razor.

Selkirk had no gun on him. "What do you want?" he asked.

"Out!" the man grunted, pointing to the door.

Selkirk's gaze returned to the smashed bowl. He was appalled, for he had no way of making such a loss good. Then his eye fixed on the raw bright edges of the pottery where it had cracked and his chin dropped.

Another man, a rifle in one hand, similar in appearance to the one standing beside him, came inside, stared at the young American.

"Out!" they both ordered.

"No. Not yet. I've got to look this over," Selkirk growled. "I'm from the town — Mr. Corellez."

They did not argue. The Indian close to him suddenly seized his arm and jerked him roughly back. "Take your hands off me," snapped Selkirk, fists clenching. He ripped away angrily, faced the bronzed man.

The latter's knife flashed out, the point was pressed under Selkirk's heart, he felt the prick of it as it passed through his shirt and cut the skin. The second Indian was swiftly on Selkirk, moccasined feet making no sound, his rifle up and cocked.

Selkirk had great natural courage but the dull, almost animal faces of the Indians worried him. They were guarding the treasure caves, and evidently had orders to allow no one to intrude.

"Out!"

Selkirk could do nothing but obey. They might, he realized, kill him if he failed to do as they told him. He walked out ahead of the two Indians, aware of the leveled rifle at his spine. He started for the faint, winding path that led to his mule below, but he was jabbed in the side by the rifle and with grunts they indicated he was to head the other way.

"But — you can't take me off like this —"
he cried. The sharp muzzle of the rifle
forced him on.

Selkirk stumbled as they pushed him up
over the rim of the crater and he found
himself on a steep slope, feet almost sliding
from under him. The dark wilderness spread
out before him in a breath-taking drop, mile
upon mile of rugged land stretching into
the night, rocks and lava, overgrown with
trees and brush, an untracked land.

Slowly he descended, and the Indian with
the knife, who had picked up another rifle
as he left the cave, led the way now, but the
other was at his back, ready evidently to
shoot if Selkirk tried to break away. He did
not like their ominous silence, nor their
fierce, untamed look.

For a time he went with them docilely.
But inside he was angry and worried. He
must get back to Voorhees — and Edith.

They swung south along a narrow, spiral-
ing terrace of the mountain. Now and then
a stone would roll under Selkirk's boot and
go bounding down the slides into the space
below.

Great rocks showed before them, gigantic
boulders large as houses. The leading Indian
swung behind one of these. Selkirk stopped
suddenly, and the rifle barrel touched his

ribs, slid between his arm and body. He turned like a flash and grappled with the man behind. The gun went off, the slug spattering against the rock face, the heat from the steel singeing Selkirk's skin.

He was a strong young athlete, however, and with a swift twist he threw back the Indian's arms, catching his opponent's fingers in the trigger guard. The man did not give any cry of pain but let go the rifle and closed with him silently, simply grunting as he strained at Selkirk. The latter had to make his play swiftly; he put all his strength into it and bore the Indian down under him, trying to escape the clutch of the nailed hands. He drove his knee into the bare belly, felt the grasp loosen. He jerked himself free, and started to run back along the way he had come.

He heard the guttural warning of the man he had knocked down. The other Indian bounded out, raised his rifle and sent a bullet that whirled close to the dark figure of Selkirk ahead. Then both came after him, their moccasined feet gripping the stony path with a sureness and speed that was impossible for Selkirk.

Both overtook him fifty yards from the great rocks and caught him from behind, knocking him down and falling upon him.

He was hit with the horn handles of their knives and then one held his legs while the other put a sharp blade to his throat.

He thought of Edith, her sweetness and blond beauty. He didn't want to die. Life was all before him.

Then they rose and kicked him up, stayed close by him, more vigilant, as they shoved him roughly to the gigantic stones. They picked up his lantern, and, after a time, among the stones, swung into a low tunnel, entrance to a cave in the side of the mountain.

The lantern lit, he was thrown down on the dry, powdered lava floor. He looked about him. There were blankets and camping things strewn about the stone chamber.

"Wait," growled one of the Indians, standing over him.

A big man, with a six-shooter gripped in his paw, came from the dark recesses of the cave. He was yawning, the black stubble bristling on his bronzed, dark face. His stringy brown hair was awry, he had been sleeping and the shots had disturbed him. His left eye was permanently half-closed by a cross-shaped knife scar. It was Gila Mike Turner, the giant bandit.

"What the hell's goin' on, Gerajo?" he

growled, addressing the Indian close to Selkirk.

Gerajo explained with a few grunting words, stretched out with gestures. Gila Mike slouched over to Selkirk.

"What yuh snoopin' up here fer, young fella?"

Selkirk was glad to have someone who would speak more than single words. "I just came up to have a look at some things in the crater caverns," he told Turner, who scowled down at him. "These Indians captured me and forced me to come here."

Gila Mike was cross as a bear that has been disturbed. "That's yore story," he snarled. "Funny yuh'd be snoopin' up here in the dark, all alone. Yuh shore yuh wasn't huntin' fer me, huh?"

He stirred Selkirk impatiently with his big boot toe.

"Of course not, I work for Hans Voorhees. D' you mind calling these Indians off, and letting me go back to town? I want to see Mr. Voorhees in the morning."

Gila Mike glowered at him. "Too many danged fools huntin' me nowadays," he insisted. "Yuh can't lie to me. I bet Cal Davis sent yuh from Brewster to catch up with me."

"No, you're wrong."

Turner kicked him viciously. "Don't call me a liar, yuh spang-nosed dude," he snarled. "Tie him up, Gerajo. And, Manino, yuh watch him and if he tries to git away, give him yore knife."

"But you can't do this," cried Bert angrily. "I'll tell Corellez and Voorhees, they'll send Marshal Crole after you. You have no right to hold me a prisoner. I haven't done anything to you, and I've got to see Voorhees."

"Why?"

Selkirk hesitated. Gila Mike gave a hoarse laugh. "Thinkin' up a yarn, huh? Well, nuthin' doin', sport. Yuh won't git a chanct to lead Crole nor no other hombres up here after me. I'm tired of dodgin' and this is the on'y place I kin feel safe. Now yuh've horned in and so Gawd help yuh."

The giant outlaw's brutal face was close to Selkirk's. Bert saw in this man's cruel intelligence a much more dangerous enemy than in the animal-like Indians.

"I — I wanted to warn Voorhees."

" 'Bout what?"

Bert shook his head. He had been sworn to secrecy as to the Aztec find. Gila Mike was obviously a criminal and Selkirk did not wish to expose the value of what was in those caves to such a man.

The lantern still burned low. Gerajo, the first Indian, had produced rawhide bonds and was tying them so tightly on Bert's wrists and ankles that the circulation was cut off.

Gila Mike sneered at Selkirk again, swung and went into the dark recesses of the cave, saying that he'd see what to do with the dude in the morning. Manino, standing near the entrance of the cavern, suddenly gave a grunt.

"Reach, gents!" said a level, quiet voice.

CHAPTER IX
TREASURE

Jim Hatfield, six-gun cocked in his big hand, loomed in the cave entry. He stared curiously at the frozen figures of the two Indians, Gerajo still bent over by Selkirk, and Manino close at his right.

Beyond the circle of the light he did not see the dark form of Gila Mike as the giant bandit turned, pistol rising.

"Look out! There's a gunman back there," cried Selkirk.

As Selkirk spoke, Manino leaped at Hatfield, his long knife flashing in a swift downward arc. The Ranger caught the Indian's wrist on his gun arm, turning the tearing point aside, though it ripped a chunk from his sleeve, scratched him.

Gila Mike's gun boomed in the cave. The Ranger's bullet, deflected by the swift Indian's leap, burrowed into the rock ceiling. Turner's slug caught Manino in the side, under the heart, and the Indian died in Hatfield's clutch, his dead weight dragging the Ranger to his knees. Gila Mike's second slug ripped two inches over Hatfield's Stetson crown and tore through the door into the outer air, to end up in the rocks.

Hatfield, holding up the dead Indian as a shield, sent a hot round of bullets that made Gila Mike duck for cover. Blinded by the lantern, the Ranger cursed as he heard the swiftly diminishing steps of the gunman who had greeted him with hot lead.

"Who's that shootin' back there, d'yuh know?" he called to Bert Selkirk.

"A man with a cross scar on his face!"

"Gila Mike!"

Hatfield did not wait for further identification, he plowed forward letting Manino's body slip to the ground. Gerajo, with a terrible cry at seeing Manino limp in death, leaped to his rifle, black eyes blazing furious hatred. He blamed the big Ranger for the death of his brother. Selkirk rolled over, bound legs flashing out, tripping Gerajo as he swung the rifle on the Lone Wolf.

The Ranger was running after Gila Mike, oblivious to the Indian. But, hearing Selkirk's warning shout, he swung and sent a slug that seared the Indian's gun arm and sent him dashing from the cavern.

Hatfield ran on, into the darkness of the cave. He paused an instant, listening, and heard far ahead the sounds of a man moving. He fired a shot but it plunked into the bulge of the wall ten yards ahead. The cave passage narrowed down, and under a ledge he saw the blankets where Turner had been sleeping.

He shoved on, feeling his way with his left hand. The air that hit his face was cool and damp — a draught. In the sheer blackness he bumped against an overhanging rock. He struck a match, which flared up, showing the winding passage he was in. It was barely wide enough to let a big man through, a honeycomb in the side of Bald Top.

As the match flickered out, a bullet spat within an inch of his ear, knocking bits of rock into his eyes. Gila Mike was up ahead there. The Ranger went on.

Presently he saw stars ahead, the lesser darkness of the powdery sky. He was sure that Gila Mike had ducked out this opening.

The Ranger slowed down, gun cocked and ready, creeping toward the hole through which he was sure the giant outlaw had disappeared. Turner might be lying outside, just waiting for him to stick his head through.

Cautiously he stuck out his Stetson on the end of his pistol. It was immediately blown off the gun barrel, but Hatfield had discovered Gila Mike's position, the flash showed the shot came from directly above the hole out of which the Ranger must leap in order to trail Turner.

It seemed like certain death to make that jump, but Hatfield gathered his powerful muscles. He would dive out, whirl and try to get Gila Mike as he turned.

Suddenly he heard Gila Mike utter a startled curse. Something struck Hatfield a heavy, glancing blow in the shoulder, nearly cracking it and knocking him flat on his right hip. It was as though he had been hit by a giant hand and brushed aside as if he were a fly.

A dull rumble was followed by a cloud of dirt that clogged the Ranger's eyes and nostrils. He realized that an immense rock overhanging the hole had collapsed, probably from Gila Mike's weight on it as he crouched. A corner had bruised Hatfield's shoulder, and he had rolled backward. The small exit was now all but blocked by the rock and dirt. Hatfield, striking a match in the dust-filled air, realized it would take him an hour to make a passageway.

He turned and went back the way he had come. He could see the faint lantern light as he neared them. Selkirk still lay there, but Gerajo was gone and when the Ranger made a hurried survey outside, he did not see or hear Gila Mike or the Indian. There were a thousand hiding places, and Hatfield was not yet acquainted with the lay of the land, for he had only that evening ridden in from the southwest, having circled below Bald Top in order to get up on the mountain without being observed by those in Corellez. His only reason for coming was that he had seen the lantern dancing along the mountain crest, then heard the shots. The latter had made him decide to investigate.

It took him but a couple of moments to pick up Manino's knife and cut the rawhides binding Bert Selkirk.

"Mighty fine of you to save me, sir," said Selkirk, greatly relieved.

The big Ranger looked at Selkirk narrowly. Cunningly shrewd in his diagnoses of most men, he had liked the young man's square shoulders and manly air. There was nothing noisy about Selkirk, and, though he was a tenderfoot in the Southwest and certainly not a gun-fighter, he had a good strong jaw and determined, intelligent eyes.

Hatfield, squatting with back to the stone wall, facing the cave door, listened for any false note that might creep into the man's voice. With the other ear he waited for warning sounds which might announce the return of Gila Mike and the Indian Gerajo. The white ivories of Manino, gritted in death, glistened in the yellow lantern light.

"I don't know whether they were going to kill me or not," Selkirk told him, but there wasn't any undue panic or fear in his tone. He had kept his nerve well, despite the manhandling and threats of Gila Mike and the Indians. "But they sure meant to keep me prisoner. I'm obliged to you because it means a great deal for me — and others — that I can get back down to Corellez right away." His clear gaze sought the Ranger's steady eyes.

"Yes, yuh can git back, but what's yore hurry?"

Selkirk hesitated, and the Ranger did not miss the furrowing of his forehead.

"Better tell me," Hatfield said briefly.

There was command in the deep voice. Though the grey-green eyes were deep with power, they did not frighten Selkirk, but rather drew him, forced him to trust the mighty Lone Wolf. The Ranger's personality was chilling as death to the evil doer, but it offered protection to decent people. Selkirk was fascinated by the rugged lines of the man's stern face, the sureness and decision of his actions as he had fought the Indians and Gila Mike.

"I will," Selkirk said slowly, "because I'm positive I can count on you. I don't know who or what you are but you're aces with me. I saw you in Brewster and in Corellez, too. I promised that I wouldn't disclose any secrets of this place, but after what's happened I think I can safely tell you everything."

Rapidly he began to tell Hatfield how he came to be down in that far country. As Dr. Wallace Jackson's assistant he had accompanied Professor Jackson, met Hans Voorhees and Edith, his daughter. The Ranger didn't miss the expression in Bert Selkirk's eyes as the young man mentioned the girl.

"Voorhees invited us to come down with

him and look at a new Aztec find," Selkirk informed the Ranger. "Cassius Green — he's the little, dried-up man you may have noticed — was also asked. Voorhees agreed to pay expenses and a fee as well, though the interest of it to us was well worth the time and trouble. George Vance, who's an expedition field man, was the third Voorhees brought with him, to help decide the authenticity and value of the treasure."

"Jest what is this treasure?"

"Aztec relics, jewel-decorated utensils and weapons, of great archeological value. They were stored here in these caverns almost four hundred years ago by fleeing subjects of Montezuma, who sent them far off from his capital of Tenochititlan, the ancient site on which now stands modern Mexico City. Mosaic, gold ornaments, topaz, jade, agate, amethyst, quartz, emeralds and diamonds too, were used in their beautiful art. The obsidian or volcanic glass work is most remarkable, unequalled." Selkirk's eyes shone with enthusiasm as he told the Ranger of the interesting Aztecs. He painted vivid word-pictures of the aboriginal tribes of Mexico whose great empire had been so cruelly smashed by Cortez.

"So that's it," Hatfield drawled musingly. Now he understood the secrecy — some of it. If they had found such a trove they wouldn't want others horning in, running around to take their trinkets. But there were other angles that puzzled him. Where did Gila Mike fit into the mosaic of Corellez?

"But," Selkirk went on, eyes clouding, "I gave my approval this afternoon. Not that it meant much because I'm only an advanced student. My friend, Dr. Jackson, has taught me all I know about antiquities, and he was wounded in Brewster, the night you arrested the gunmen who shot him. He would never, I'm sure, have given such a snap judgment as we did, Green and Vance and I. You see, I got to thinking it over, and realized I'd only handled a few pieces and they were all good, genuine. Jackson had said so himself."

"And Voorhees?"

"Well, Voorhees knows very little, you see. He's a gambler, he buys such collections and then resells them. He's pretty careful, which is why he brought along Jackson, Green and Vance — Vance isn't an expert, but he's very interested in Aztec stuff, and knows a great deal about their work. He joined us at Austin on our way down."

"But this here Green ought to know his business?"

Selkirk nodded. "He does. But — well, I came up here myself tonight, to look more carefully at the relics. Mr. Voorhees is paying a huge sum for the collection to Corellez, who discovered it, and dug it out. I had hardly got started inspecting the treasure when I was jumped by those Indian devils and brought down here. Then that big man told me I'd have to stay."

The Ranger nodded. "Those are Apaches. Best trackers in the world, Selkirk." He knew now for sure who had tried to creep in on him, that night when he had camped in the brush on first riding into the wild mountains.

Gerajo and Manino, undoubtedly, coming up to look him over, maybe to cut his throat. They could move like shadows in their moccasins, and they could travel miles on foot, at a swift dogtrot, needing no horses, going long intervals without water or food, the greatest foot soldiers and trailsmen ever known.

He was still watching Selkirk, the troubled look in the young man's eyes. The more Selkirk talked, the better impression he gave the shrewd Ranger.

"I'm not used to fighting with guns and knives," admitted Selkirk. "Maybe I'm not fitted for this job."

"Yuh'll do to ride the river with," the Ranger informed him soberly.

It was a high compliment and though Selkirk didn't altogether understand its import — that a man who could be trusted to help another to push a frightened cattle herd over a flooded river, was an A-1 citizen — he nodded gratefully.

"I'd better get back to Corellez and see Mr. Voorhees."

The Ranger asked why.

"You see, when that Apache sneaked up behind me with his knife, I was so startled I dropped a bowl I was holding, and it broke. That's what's got me so worried. The color and condition of the inner clay seems too new to be ancient Aztec. But — it's just that one bowl, of course, and maybe I'm wrong."

Hatfield's eyes widened and he contemplated Selkirk for a moment. "Huh!"

"He wasn't," thought Selkirk, "much more communicative than the Apaches. And in comparative deadliness, the young Easterner felt he would much rather face in a fight a whole tribe of the taciturn Indians than this supple-muscled, very crafty Western lawman.

Hatfield drew forth the makin's, rolled a cigarette. For a long while he remained squatted on his haunches, obviously thinking it all over. In the silence of the cave, a distant, vague voice startled Selkirk and he looked quickly all around, trying to place it. The voice seemed like that of a ghost speaking from a distant world.

"Mike!" it whined. "Mike!" it called again and there was a metallic quality about it.

CHAPTER X
CAPTURED!

The Ranger straightened up, dropping his cigarette and crushing it under his riding boot. His big hand ordered Selkirk to be quiet, and they listened.

"Mike!"

Hatfield swung back toward the spot where Gila Mike had been sleeping, the lantern in his fingers. He saw a crevice in the wall of the cavern and then noted the end of an iron pipe hidden in the vertical crack. From this the faint voice came.

"Turner — Mike!" Someone wanted Gila Mike in a hurry.

Hatfield put his mouth to the pipe. The tube so distorted a voice with whistling air that he did not believe his own would be recognized at the far end. He spoke gruffly.

"Hi up there! This is Mike, whatcha want?"

"Mike, I'm in a hurry. Have you seen anything of that fool Selkirk? He's sneaked out of the camp."

"No. Ain't seen him," said Hatfield.

"He's not in the cavern now, but someone's been here. We've about won, Mike, and we can't take any chances. Stay on guard up here the rest of the night. If you catch Selkirk, hold him."

"I savvy. Wait for me, I'll be right up."

"Haven't time, I must get back. See you tomorrow. And Mike, there's some things I want you to do."

"Okay, Boss."

The whistling voice ceased. Hatfield swung on Selkirk.

"C'mon, yuh go down and tell Voorhees not to close any deal till yuh hear from me. And keep outa sight of Corellez and his hombres, savvy?" Hatfield pounded home his warning.

"Where are *you* going?" asked Selkirk.

The Ranger's grey-green eyes were sombre. "Goin' to find what this is all about," he replied.

"I'd sure feel better if you were along with me."

"Yuh don't wanta be seen with me jest now. Hustle down to town, and warn Voorhees!"

There was a six-gun hanging in a cartridge belt from a wooden peg driven into the wall over the rough bed where Gila Mike had been lying when Selkirk was brought in. Evidently an extra one the bandit had been in too great a hurry to seize. The Ranger stepped over and took it down, and his boot toe caught in the blanket, and kicked it aside. The Lone Wolf paused, staring down at a metal edge which peeped up from the loose grey silt. He stooped and brushed away some of the powdered rock.

Close to the surface were rows of silver bars. Hatfield scooped away more of the finely-powdered rock and beside the bars were canvas bags containing silver dollars.

The Ranger straightened and silently handed Selkirk the spare gun and belt. The young easterner strapped it around his lean waist and there was determination shining in his eyes. His new strength came from the Ranger's coolness and bravery.

"I'll get to Voorhees," he announced. "We're not sure yet, but this all looks suspicious. I never did like Corellez's looks."

Hatfield nodded, blew out the lantern and led the way out into the starry night. Far below, to the west, Goldy was picketed, waiting his return. But to ride around the Bald Top mountain would take many hours and the descent to Corellez could be accomplished much more swiftly by crossing the crater and going directly down the steep trail.

They followed the narrow, winding ledge to the rim of the crater, climbed over and went down inside. The wind whined across the top of the mighty hole and whipped them along.

Selkirk led the way to the entrance of the treasure cave and gave Hatfield his oil-lantern. The Ranger made a light and soon Selkirk was hurrying to where he had left his mule. The animal was waiting patiently and he mounted and headed down the precipitous way, which would take him back to Corellez. He hoped that he would be in time to stop Hans Voorhees from purchasing what was beginning to have the earmarks of a doubtful find.

Anxiety was upon him but Selkirk braced himself. There was, after all, a possibility he might be mistaken. Professor Green had okayed the Aztec deposits and Green knew his business. So did George Vance, who was certainly a most intelligent man, and had been with Voorhees on a previous trip. Then again Vance had done a great deal of prospecting in the Southwest. But a delay of another day, while the treasures were checked further, could do no harm.

He drew in a deep breath of the fragrant mountain air. The slight rustlings in the brush, and the deep shadows of the deformed arms of gnarled trees, kept his ears and eyes busy, for he was sure that someone might try to prevent his return to Corellez.

There was a faint hint of grey in the eastern quadrant of the sky when Bert Selkirk saw before him the shacks of the Camp. Eagerly he pressed forward. Edith occupied one of the huts. Selkirk felt that what he was doing was for her as well as for the sake of his old mentor, Dr. Jackson.

Passing the last line of the brush, and heading across the flat of the gap floor, he jerked suddenly on his rein, stopping the mule short. He saw the dark shadows of men before him, rising menacingly between him and the hut where Voorhees was staying.

They had seen him emerge from the bush, and an instant later they started at him. He guessed their intention, and his hand dropped to the butt of the pistol which the Ranger had pressed on him.

"There he is!" Gila Mike's rough voice growled. "Git him, quick, boys! Don't let him yell none, the dirty skunk!"

Selkirk jerked his reins, pivoting the mule to retreat.

Gila Mike and his followers threw themselves on their ponies, made a concerted rush for Selkirk, as the young man beat the mule.

"Mr. Voorhees!" bawled Bert. He'd try to warn the old collector if he died in the attempt!

Turner opened fire on his retreating figure. The slugs whistled close about Selkirk, cut the brush near at hand as the mule plunged into the thickets. A bullet drilled into the animal's hind leg, laming it immediately, and it began to buck and leap about, screeching in pain. Selkirk clung to the rocketing saddle.

The giant bandit and his hombres came rushing at him. A lariat whistled through the air and settled over Bert's shoulders as he tried to answer their fire with his pistol. He was yanked bodily from the saddle and fell with a thud to the stony earth.

"Mr. Voorhees!" shrieked Selkirk, desperately. "Edith — be careful. Don't —"

Gila Mike fell upon him, ramming a knee into his stomach and gripping Selkirk's throat with his huge hands. The bandit banged Bert's head against a rock, then shook him furiously.

"Vot's going on oudt dere?" It was Dutch Voorhees, aroused by Selkirk's yells.

"Bandits — bandits!" another man cried loudly. "Where's Crole? Marshal, quick, Gila Mike!"

Gila Mike, cruel face twisted, lifted Selkirk as though the stalwart young man were a child and slung him across a saddle. He mounted behind, and followed by twenty riders, headed into the bush. In a few hours they hoped to reach Bald Top.

"Yuh'll git yores," Gila Mike snarled, clouting Selkirk viciously.

While Bert Selkirk rode down the mountain toward violent death, Ranger Jim Hatfield burrowed deep into the treasure caverns of the Aztecs.

He reconnoitred carefully before entering the twelve-foot-high opening, he was ready for trouble, but none came. The wind whined overhead, small puffs of white clouds scudding in the night sky. He had expected a gun welcome, but so far everything had been peaceful. He drew no bullets or attack as he went in the dark cave.

Hatfield made no attempt to conceal his arrival. He walked into the cave, his heels making a hollow ringing sound on the hard cavern floor. He struck a match holding it out from his body to see if it would be used as a target by lurking foes. But there was no sharp rifle crack; instead there was a sharp whirring of wings and a frightened bat whirled past knocking the match from his hand.

The Ranger lit another and touched it to the wick of Selkirk's lantern. Several more of the bats terrified by the light flew past his head, out into the open.

Curiously he looked about him, at the piles of stuff lining the walls. There were big bales and rough tables on which stood hundreds of objects, ornaments and knives with carved handles. The broken bowl which Selkirk had mentioned had been picked up and taken away, undoubtedly by the man who had called down through that pipe to Gila Mike.

He advanced on into the cave, glancing at the collection set forth. The cavern was large and there were large masses of uneven volcanic rock that rose up in the floor making the footing uneven.

It took him five minutes to locate the upper outlet of the pipe, driven down through a crevice. It was well hidden at this end, but he found the speaking-tube behind the bulge of a jutting rock, covered by a hanging blanket. It had been driven down through a fissure in the cave to Gila Mike's den below and was a handy way for the

"Boss" to give his henchman orders.

The Ranger began to inspect the dust-covered treasures. The collection of ancient weapons, fancy hilts of knives and swords, and abundant mosaics were beautifully made. There were scattered objects encrusted with all sorts of shining stones; rawhide war shields, and many figures of the Aztec gods, of War and the Sun-Chief; of Xipe, the Flayed One, and the Plumed Serpent — Hatfield could identify various commonly known Mexican gods.

Musical instruments, and several calendar stones with intricate carving, interested him greatly. The arrows, and Indian birds in jewels, and ever present the delicately worked black obsidian called something faintly to mind. The Aztecs had used it for knife blades, and set it as teeth in their strange swords with jeweled hilts —

He turned various objects over and over in his long, brown hands.

"Some of it's mighty purty," he murmured, impressed by the minute workmanship. Then he took the end of his bandanna and began to rub the outer base of a dull yellow bowl, set with green stones that glinted like emeralds.

Soon small yellow flakes came off on his bandanna. He held the bowl close to the lantern and put his eyes almost against it, to inspect the faint scratches that he had uncovered on its uneven flat bottom.

His long eyes narrowed. He set the bowl down carefully, and went to another piece.

It took time to look over the large collection in the cavern. When he had finished, the cave mouth showed grey, for dawn was close at hand.

"Now I savvy," he muttered. "Lucky I know of that trademark! Makes me dead certain!"

Hatfield's mouth was determinedly set. He blew out the lantern and started for the exit. He left carefully, pausing in the uneven doorway and looking around as far as he could see.

There was a pile of broken rock to the left, and directly in front several large, flat stones. Up a slope, ahead, he could see the half-collapsed crater wall. To the right the side of the wall curved and cut off his vision.

The Lone Wolf decided that he must hurry and get down to Corellez in order to back up Bert Selkirk. He was sure of his ground, since he had seen the treasure, and Selkirk's suspicions were well grounded.

Suddenly he leaped backward, almost falling in his speed. The black muzzle of a rifle had jutted out from a right-hand bulwark and he saw the glowing Apache eyes of Gerajo. An instant later, a blinding flash burst almost in Hatfield's face, as the .30-30 bullet cut a hole in his shirt, and spanged against the rock wall.

The Ranger made his blindingly fast draw, six-gun blaring back at the Apache Gerajo, who jumped sideways, as a line of heads appeared around the crater rim and the whole face of the cave was covered with a fusillade of slugs. The Ranger rolled behind the protection of the Aztec treasure piles, as he glimpsed the burly head of Gila Mike Turner. The giant bandit had evidently brought plenty of reinforcements, and they had the Ranger Jim Hatfield trapped inside the cave.

He sent a swift shot at Gila Mike but the range was too long for accurate fire with a pistol, and his bullet spurted dust a foot below the murderous rustler. In reply the rifles crackled again, the bullets either hitting the sides or entering the cavern to be stopped by the rock walls.

They did not charge him but contented themselves with holding him where he was. The sun cast red fingers into the crater, and the small patch of sky that the Ranger could see was a beautiful turquoise hue. Hatfield could hear Gila Mike's raucous laughter.

"Hi, in there!" Turner bawled. "How yuh like *my* jail, Mister Depitty? C'mon, try to git outa it. Better'n Brewster lock-up, huh?"

Hatfield did not reply to the torrent of abuse the bandits hurled at him. But one thing was evident; Gila Mike still believed he had been sent down there by Sheriff Davis of Brewster. The Texas Rangers had not entered the bandit's mind.

They cursed him, and dared him to show himself. Hatfield, in the meanwhile, went farther into the bowels of the cavern, relit the lantern and made his way down the sloping floor. The cave wound this way and that, deeper into the crater.

It was many centuries since old Bald Top had erupted and time had aged and softened the volcanic interior. Water had seeped in, carrying calcium salts, to form strangely-shaped deposits. Dust and dirt had blown through, bats and other animals left their traces.

After a time there were no more Aztec objects lining the walls. The Ranger kept on along a narrowing way that led deeper into the caves. There were chambers widening out here and there. Then without warning Hatfield was up to his knees in icy water so still and clear that it looked like a continuation of the floor.

The pool deepened and ended against a wall. The Ranger searched its surface for a crevice or opening, but there was nothing but massive rock. Hatfield was cut off. The only way out of the treasure cave was the entrance covered by the hungry guns of Gila Mike.

"Then that's the way we go," Hatfield muttered, as he turned.

He refilled his six-guns, and rapidly made his way to the upper cavern. The sound of rocks grinding together hastened his steps, and then he saw a gang of tough hombres rolling giant stones and rubble to close the opening. They were meaning to entomb him. Already the pile they had made was as high as the Ranger's head.

A rapid fire from his pistols scattered the workers, one shrieked as a bullet tore through his shoulder, spinning him in a half circle. He fell off the rock pile, as Gila Mike's guns boomed and echoed.

Most of their slugs spat on the rocks they themselves had piled up, affording the Ranger some protection. A hand against the newly shifted stones, he leaned forward, with a couple of shots, drove them back out of sight. But there were still riflemen on the crater edge, who could pick him off if he climbed over in full sight. But he must get out. His rugged jaw set.

"Ain't much time," he growled as he peered up at the patch of sky.

Smoke balls from the guns floated away to the left. That meant the wind blew that way, though it wasn't very violent.

Hatfield hurried back into the inner cave. He found plenty of canvas tarpaulins and some wooden storage boxes, which he emptied of their contents. There was still some kerosene oil in the lantern and he poured it on the wood and canvas. With a long stick he pushed the material through to the windward side of the rocks, unmindful of the spattering of the bandit bullets.

He lit the oil-soaked lantern wick and tossed it on the pile. The kerosene flared and flames licked upward, and the stuff began to blaze. Fire was trapped under the heavy canvas sheets and thick black smoke billowed out on the breeze.

The Ranger climbed over the stone barricade and leaped down hidden by the smoke-pall. The choking breath of the fire caught at his throat but he swung rapidly, and leaped for the jutting side which would give him protection from the riflemen on the crater lip.

"Git him, there he goes!" Gila Mike had

glimpsed the tall figure as it flitted through the heavy smoke screen.

Rifle bullets whirled at him, but Hatfield rushed on.

A shriek sounded close to the Ranger's left, as he jumped for the projecting stone column. Gila Mike's bullets had hit one of his own men, one of those who had been piling the stones.

"Careful, Mike!" bawled an hombre close to the Ranger.

Then Hatfield's six-guns began to boom. He slugged the barrel across the twisted face of a black-bearded bandit who rose up before him, clubbed rifle swinging to smash the Ranger to earth. The man went down and Hatfield stamped his gun-hand with a heavy boot. A bullet from the Lone Wolf's six-shooter tore into a second killer's face, and he crashed. He was dead before he landed.

Then Hatfield leaped for shelter, as the others split and flew like buzzards when an eagle lands among them. The Ranger hurried behind big boulders scattered along the ledge, while his six-shooters sent the stampeded gunmen on their way.

But he did not wait long for Gila Mike and the hombres from the crater lip were charging forward, yelling in fury and shooting through the drifting smoke. The Ranger scuttled back around the bulge in the crater formed by the roof of the cavern. At full tilt he ran for the down trail and was well on his way before Gila Mike and his gang came up on the lip. He lunged forward, as their lead whistled close over his body.

Now he was in the undergrowth, able to duck this way and that as they pursued him, scattering out to surround him. The Ranger held his fire and doggedly pushed downhill, boots sliding on the rough ground.

"What's up, Mike?" a man yelled.

The hail came from the Ranger's left and he swung toward it, body low as he advanced. A man smoking a cigarette stood there guarding the saddled mules and ponies. He was staring up, his attention riveted to Gila Mike's men in pursuit of the Lone Wolf. He called a second time to Gila Mike.

Hatfield leaped out upon him. He recognized the man as one of Corellez' supposed miners; he had seen him in the Silver Steer Saloon.

"Why, what the hell — ?" gasped his enemy, hand flying to his six-shooter, as he realized who was coming at him.

The pistol cleared leather but never went

off. Hatfield's .45 Colt leveled him; then the Ranger was in a saddle, his barking gun breaking the bunched mounts and scattering them before him. His own mule, ears back flat, startled by the gun-fire trotted swiftly down the brushy, winding trail toward Corellez.

Gila Mike and his gun men would have to chase their mules and mountain poines first before trailing the Ranger. Hatfield gained a few hundred yards, before he heard their angry cries and he must have been well on the trail headed for the camp below before the first man drew rein.

Making good time the Ranger entered the gap, and trotted the mule toward the big saloon. The sun was well up, over the top of the mountain and was blazing into the narrow mountain valley.

Hatfield saw neither Bert Selkirk nor Hans Voorhees, but a train of pack mules and saddled ponies stood outside the saloon. Men were busy tightening bellybands and cinches; some were adjusting loads.

Marshal Crole, seated on the edge of the saloon porch, with a cigarette drooping from his lips, suddenly recognized the battered Hatfield riding toward him. He was facing Bald Top, had heard the shooting, and evidently wondered what it was about.

He leaped to his feet. "Hey, Corellez!" he bawled.

The grey, gaunt town boss hurried from the door of the Silver Steer before the ranger rode up. The saloon was crowded with men, those who had been employed in the caverns, supposedly digging out the Aztec treasures.

Hatfield leaped off the mule's back and faced Crole. The marshal's bulging eyes fixed on him. Fear was written in those eyes. Corellez hesitated an instant, his grey face glowering at the Lone Wolf.

The hitch-rail was lined with horses. The Ranger, eyes always on Crole and his employer, barked a question. "Where's Voorhees?"

The marshal gulped. "Why — uh —" His eyes strayed from the steady gaze that pierced him and made him go cold. Suddenly they flickered. There was a mighty pounding of horses' feet. Gila Mike and his hombres came charging, howling, from the mountain trail.

"Gila Mike! Bandits," shrieked Corellez, and fired a swift shot that burned along Hatfield's left forearm.

Hatfield missed Corellez as the latter fell backward into the saloon, yelling for help. Then, from the side of his eye, the Ranger saw the marshal's draw, and managed to shift his gun in time to send a slug through Crole's right shoulder. The marshal's arm dropped limp at his side, his bullet spurting dust at Hatfield's feet.

"Don't kill me please, mister," he begged. "Don't — !"

There was a rush of gunmen from the Silver Steer. The supposed treasure-hunters now hustled with rifles and pistols. Ranger Jim Hatfield was their target!

Chapter XI
Running Battle

The Ranger jumped. He had to move fast or be filled with lead from the concerted fire of his enemies. Corellez was still yelling about the arrival of Gila Mike.

Edith Voorhees hearing the firing rushed out of a nearby shack. Her face became pale as she stood, staring at the bullet-spattered scene. The choking dust rose in clouds under the stumping hoofs of the excited ponies, and gunsmoke adding to the mist. Bullets from the Silver Steer plugged into the bodies of saddled horses that stood between the Ranger and the gang on the porch, that were urged on by Corellez.

"Get Gila Mike!" urged Corellez.

And Gila Mike, fifteen desperate killers riding with him, was spurring from the northwest toward Hatfield, to hem him in. More gunmen ran from the pack-train, so that the north path was completely blocked. Hatfield's keen eyes figured out their blockade.

The Ranger seized the reins of a saddled horse, expert eye hurriedly picking a long-legged pinto. He ran, dragging the horse around the side of the Silver Steer, his bullets milling the bunched gun-fighters on the porch. Those in front felt the whistle of his lead and backed up on the toes of men behind them, ruining their aim.

Gila Mike and his bandits swept toward the saloon, but the Ranger mounted, and the pinto was off like a streak. As the swift paint horse ran, a burst of gunfire followed; the long-legged pony gave a sharp forward bound, then steadied into a fast, even gallop. The trail north was blocked by the men of the pack-train, and their pistols were out and ready. The only way to go was southward, and Hatfield took it.

Wind whistled about the Lone Wolf's long body as he drove the paint horse south. Scattered shots still screamed by him, and Gila Mike's bunch swung after him.

The gunmen would not give up but trailed

him, keeping up a long-range fight. Hatfield picked off one man and unhorsed a second with his accurate fire, and then the bandits let him gain, simply riding his drag for two miles.

As he rode, looking back now and then at the murderers who sought to finish him and prevent him from doing his duty, he turned the situation over in his alert mind. Fatigued as his body was, he still could think keenly. The many battles that he had fought and won had keened his ingenuity and strength. This encounter was just another test of the Lone Wolf's amazing power.

But Bert Selkirk's fate bore heavily upon him; he felt responsible for the young student's life. Selkirk might already be dead. Then there was the pretty Edith Voorhees and her father, whose money Corellez was after.

George Vance and Dr. Green were the only two left of the original Voorhees party; they would be able to offer scant resistance to the mob controlled by Corellez.

Gila Mike? The Ranger shrugged. Turner, he was now sure, had more than a chance rustling connection with the town boss. Corellez and Crole, sending Hatfield off on that wild-goose chase, had simply wished to get him out of the way, so they could complete the plan of selling to Voorhees that collection up on Bald Top.

They had wished Hatfield to give them a clean slate if and when he returned to Brewster. But they made the mistake of believing him a simple deputy sheriff. Had they known he was Jim Hatfield, Texas Ranger, they would have pulled down the rawplank town of Corellez and faded into the desert.

It was a dark mystery and a bloody one, but the brilliant rays of the Ranger's mind gradually lightened crevice after crevice. Wholesale murder and thievery had been done, and he was determined to make the perpetrators pay.

To his right bulked the high shoulders of great Bald Top, the extinct volcano's humpy base falling in a series of graduated red buttes, black lava slides on lower level. Green and yellow brush covered the flanks, and the black lava, with gashes of red clay precipices, made a moving scene.

Ahead, lay rough chaparral country undulating as the north and south gap culminated in broken and gigantic spews of boulders bigger than houses. To the east, on the Ranger's left hand, that other mountain stretched out like a monstrous comb thrown down by giants.

He was crossing that petrified lava river when the pinto suddenly went lame. Expert horseman that he was Hatfield realized immediately that the right rear leg of the mustang was failing — failing badly. The pinto was wet with sweat, sides heaving; he did not have Goldy's natural endurance and intelligence, and he was hurt. Hatfield wished fervently he had the yellow horse under him now, as he swung to look again at Gila Mike and his nest of hornets.

The great bandit chieftain and a dark-faced hombre, with bristling, crossed cartridge belts, were already on the lava field in the van of the pursuit. They were maddened at the tall trouble Hatfield had made for them, and thirsted for his blood.

The Ranger's eye dropped to the long, sleek muscles of the pinto's hind leg, and as the cords rippled he saw the welling blood. A bullet must have clipped the animal as they sped out of Corellez, then; that sudden jump and spurt had been the moment the paint horse had been hit. The stiffening of the muscles had finally lamed the mount.

From comparative safety and a chance to outride the killers, Hatfield was plunged by this act of fate into immediate danger of death. He might lie in a nest of rocks and hold them off for hours with his steady fire; but Gila Mike and gun-fighters would eventually outnumber him. A stick of dynamite would blow him out, anyway.

He suspected he was the last hope of the victims back there — Selkirk and Edith and her father, Hans Voorhees. His main chance would be that the pinto might last till he could reach Goldy; a detour of hours, but necessary now.

Hatfield swung on, into an arroyo, dry bed of what was a stream in rainy seasons. When he came up out of it three hundred yards farther along, the dirt sliding beneath the straining, gasping pinto's hoofs, Gila Mike and his gunmen were just dropping down into the depression.

The Ranger had ridden through here when he had circled back, after allowing Crole to believe he was headed east in search of a non-existent hideout of Gila Mike Turner. It had been tough going, across that untracked, rough mountain country.

Close to the faint trail Goldy had left as he had smashed through on the way around to Bald Top's western face, the Ranger found himself suddenly cut off in front as Gerajo the Apache broke from the track on his right, bent low over the arched neck of a golden horse.

"Goldy!" exclaimed the Ranger.

Gerajo had obviously come upon Goldy, left below when the Lone Wolf climbed to aid Bert Selkirk, and helped himself to Hatfield's pet horse. The Apaches, swift as they were afoot, knew a good horse when they saw one.

The bronzed Indian was as surprised to see Hatfield here as the latter to see Goldy. He slashed Goldy in the tender nose with a cruel quirt. The yellow horse's wide, pink nostrils flared but he obeyed, as Gerajo quickly unshipped a Winchester .30-30 rifle from the boot and took aim at the Ranger.

That long bullet whirled within inches of Hatfield's low-bent head. The Ranger had only a six-gun and it would take him moments to ride within fair range. Besides this he was poorly mounted, and his aim would be spoiled by the suffering pinto trying to cover rough terrain.

"Yip-ee! We got him now!" It was Gila Mike's roar of delight as he saw his Apache scout blocking the narrow way.

"Goldy! Goldy!" shouted Hatfield. "Buck, Goldy! Buck, old boy!"

He dug spurs into the pinto's flanks. The horse spurted forward in a terrific leap.

141

Goldy sunfished, hind hoofs almost touching his front ones in response to his master's shouted order. He began to crowhop as he came down, his head between his forelegs. No one could have fired an accurate shot from his back now and the Apache's second bullet missed Hatfield by yards.

Gerajo was forced to fight the horse to prevent himself from being thrown off. The Indian's powerful knees gripped the saddle as he quirted Goldy furiously, trying to control the powerful golden animal.

"Keep buckin', Goldy," Hatfield cried, but he would not chance a shot that might nick the sorrel.

The wind whistled past him as he charged at Gerajo, whose white teeth gleamed. The pinto collided with the bucking Goldy and Hatfield's mighty arm swept Gerajo from the saddle, breaking the Apache's grip on the leather. Then he flung Gerajo off Goldy, as the sorrel bellowed a greeting to the Ranger.

The Apache hit the dirt and rolled as though released by coiled springs. His rifle had fallen feet from him but with the speed of light he whipped out a long knife from his belt sheath. Crouched, he was about to hurl it at the Ranger's face as Hatfield pushed close alongside Goldy, preparing to mount.

But the yellow sorrel didn't like the Indian, Gerajo. Goldy hadn't forgotten the quirt wales, some even showed blood, on his nose and rump, where the Indian had beaten him unmercifully to make him obey.

Goldy lashed out, squealing, in a terrific kick that caught Gerajo in the head. There was a sound like a cracking of cocoanut shell and Gerajo's check was passed in. The knife arm fell limp and the awful impact of Goldy's shod hoofs whirled him head over heels. He lay quiet in the grass, skull pounded by the sorrel's heavy hoofs.

All this had happened in the space of a few moments. Then Hatfield left the pinto in a bound, landing in Goldy's saddle, and the sorrel was on his way, great stride putting space between the Ranger and Gila Mike, whose disappointed curses rang on the warm air. The bullets of the gang failed to touch the Lone Wolf.

They followed Hatfield for another mile. Then, looking back, after winding through broken rocks, Hatfield saw they had turned and were heading back to Corellez.

Hatfield had a definite plan in mind as he turned Goldy south. It was evening before he reached the village of Ramon Acosta, snuggled in the low hills. Men issued quickly from the cantina as they heard the beat of hoofs, and stared at the big horseman in the dying light. Surly looks were on their faces, they were ready with guns and knives. But one suddenly recognized Hatfield and cried:

"Beeg Americano! *Como está, amigo?*"

"Good, and you?" replied Hatfield.

"Muy bueno," the Mexican replied, smiling. "Don Ramon ees at the hacienda," he told the Ranger when the latter looked searchingly about the room.

Willing hands took charge of Goldy, to rub down, feed and water the golden sorrel. The soft hum of guitars once more came from the cantina.

Hatfield walked, weary and stiff-legged, up the slope to the hacienda where he had been royally entertained on his previous visit. Don Ramon, the handsome young hidalgo, greeted him. Beyond, in the dimly-lit patio garden, Hatfield glimpsed Acosta's beautiful young wife. Her dark eyes lighted in greeting as she saw the big American.

"You are welcome, senor," murmured Don Ramon, with a courtly bow. He led Hatfield inside and they sat down together. Don Ramon clapped his hands and a peon servant entered. Food and wine were ordered for the Ranger.

Not until Hatfield had eaten would Don Ramon allow him to talk of business.

"I've found the men who killed yore brother," Hatfield told him quietly. "I traced them by the trademark that yuh say yore men put on the things that they make. These things I know are yores and I have reason to believe that they were part of the loot from Don Luis' pack-train."

Don Ramon's dark eyes glinted. His hand clenched.

"I have lived for thees moment," he said.

Chapter XII
Prisoner

When he regained consciousness, Bert Selkirk felt that every bone and muscle ached in his lithe body. He realized that he was lying in a shack, bound hand and foot by rawhide bonds, a thick bandanna gag tied around his lips. Sweat poured off him, and the oppressive heat was stifling as the sun beat down on the thin brush roof.

An armed guard sat inside the closed door, watching him, a half-empty bottle of whisky in his hand resting on one knee. Beside him his cocked pistols were ready — waiting.

As he lay there, eyes rolling, Selkirk heard the stamp of many hoofs. Vaguely he recalled, as of a fresh nightmare, the events which had brought him here. And then, dimly, he heard voices.

"Father!" Edith Voorhees called. "Are you nearly ready?"

"Yah, sure, Edith dear," Voorhees' heavy voice replied, "we stardt purty quick now."

The door opened, a man stepped inside, closed it sharply behind him. It was Corellez, the grey, pale town boss who had brought Voorhees down here to sell him the Aztec treasure.

Selkirk had not much liked the big, strange person at the start, hadn't cared for his looks. He thought Corellez slimy. But Corellez had been on good behavior then and he had not worried about him.

Now he saw Corellez in a different light. That ghastly face evidently mirrored the brains of the deadly intent behind it. Corellez was a thief and a murderer. The slight mask of amiability the big boss had assumed was now thrown aside as he glowered like a death's head at the helpless Selkirk.

Corellez squatted beside him, then he drew a revolver, cocked it, and put it against Selkirk's temple. With his left hand he began

146

to untie the bandanna gagging the East-erner.

"If yuh say one word," said Corellez icily, "I'll spatter your brains all over the floor."

Selkirk's throat and mouth were dry as a tanned, salted hide. It was all he could do to whisper responses to the questions Corellez began to put to him.

"Why did you sneak up on the mountain?" demanded Corellez.

"You know."

Corellez's eyes darkened. "Yes. To cheat me, to lie about me, you dirty squirt! You okayed that stuff yesterday, didn't yuh?"

Selkirk nodded. "I'm ashamed to say I did. Now — I'm getting surer and surer you're a damn crook!"

The sharp muzzle of the Colt jabbed him painfully in the temple. Throbs of anguish coursed through his brain.

"Nothing can stop me," Corellez growled. "You have your choice of life or death. Voorhees is heading north for Brewster shortly. His daughter wonders where you are. She wants to see you.

"I've told her you're staying here in town with Green, to safeguard the interest Voorhees is buying up in the mountain. You're going to say goodby to them and again urge Voorhees to buy the stuff."

"I won't be a party to your fraud. I'll tell Voorhees the first chance I get not to buy until a free investigation is made."

"You fool!" gritted Corellez. "You love that girl, don't you? Would you like to see her die? Can't you get it through your thick head that we'll kill every one of you rather than be exposed and lose our money?"

Panic streaked through Selkirk. He thought only of Edith. He hadn't realized fully before how completely Voorhees and Edith, the whole party, were in Corellez's power. For the first time he saw the gigantic hoax. This town was a plant, a lure to cheat Voorhees, part of the stage props set up by Corellez to make the treasure look authentic.

"I'll do what you say," he agreed, "if you don't hurt her."

"That's right. I knew you would. I'm going to untie you. Gus'll bring you a pail of water so you can wash up some. Keep yourself in hand, and don't forget to smile. Remember, the girl will suffer first if you make a mistake.

"Tell Voorhees your advice is to buy, that you're staying here till he returns from Brewster. You'll be let go after we've finished with that. And there'll be guns on you every

148

instant, and on your sweetheart, even though they won't be visible."

Selkirk thought rapidly. Hans Voorhees had no such sum of cash with him as Corellez was asking for the fake relics. It would be necessary for them to return to Brewster, where there was a bank, to cash any check Voorhees signed. Someone might be able to warn Voorhees in that time. At the moment, he had to save Edith and her father.

As though divining his thoughts, Corellez said: "We've had Green in hand ever since we got down here. He's scared out of his head."

That explained Green's behavior. And, in a clear-visioned flash, Selkirk suddenly understood the shooting of his friend Dr. Jackson in a Brewster saloon. It had been deliberately planned. They had decided Jackson couldn't be intimidated, and they were right; so they had arranged to have him safely kept in Brewster.

"Vance isn't expert enough to realize he's been fooled," Corellez drawled. "He'll go back with Voorhees."

George Vance, then, was the last chance. The field man, though not having a fund of knowledge on Indian relics, might possibly have seen through the plot, might be holding his counsel till he came to the right spot. Selkirk wished he'd thought of that; but then, he hadn't been certain until he had smashed that bowl and noted the fresh clay inside under the glazing and mosaic.

Selkirk did not envisage the fact that Voorhees, and Green, himself, all must die in order to cover the thieves completely. The pasty-faced Corellez kept that to himself.

Selkirk washed up quickly, slicked himself as best he could. Corellez gave him a drink of whisky and he braced himself and stepped out into the sunlight.

Voorhees was already mounted, and George Vance, the field man, was close by Edith, standing at the heads of their saddled horses. Vance was smiling at the pretty young woman. Her eyes were anxious as she kept looking around, but when she saw Selkirk her face lighted and she took a step forward.

"Careful now," muttered Corellez to Selkirk, gripping his arm warningly.

Selkirk was aware the big man had a hand close to his six-gun butt. A quick cry to Voorhees now might prevent them from taking their crooked profit, but it would mean instant death for the party.

"Smile," hissed Corellez.

Gunmen lounged all around them. Marshal Crole sat in the shade of the saloon porch, his right arm in a sling. Selkirk knew that Crole worked for Corellez, so it would be useless to appeal to the marshal.

He forced a smile to his bruised face.

"Bert!" Edith cried, coming to him.

"Hello, Edith. I — I fell into a prickly pear bush this morning, been trying to fix up my face ever since," he told her. He did not wish to arouse her suspicions, he wanted her to get back to safety, to Brewster.

"I hate to leave, Bert," she said, a troubled expression in her eyes, "but I've got to go with Dad. We'll be back in five or six days. I wish you were coming with us to Brewster."

"I've got to stay here and tend to things," he muttered.

Dr. Green was standing beside Voorhees, looking up at the Dutchman. His face was as yellow as a lemon, and there were dark bands under his wide eyes. He could not hide his fright, though he was in deathly fear of his captor who held him with invisible bonds.

"You look bad, Green," Voorhees remarked.

"Yes, yes. I've — uh — had a little touch of fever," Green said, almost gasping. He was almost out of his wits.

"Better take some medicine. You advise me to buy, den? Sure the relics are authentic?"

"Of course. It's the chance of a lifetime! Buy — buy quickly, by all means!"

"All right, den, we buy. Come, Edie," called Voorhees. "We got to hustle."

She walked, Selkirk at her side, to her horse. Voorhees said to Bert: "A goot thing, eh, Selkirk? We mage plenty of profit on dis deal."

"That's right," Selkirk replied levelly. "A great bargain, Mr. Voorhees." Corellez was looking at him and there was an evil smile on his lips.

"We all agree, then," George Vance cried enthusiastically. "I'm glad you think it's such a valuable find, Voorhees."

Selkirk caught the field man's gaze. He opened his eyes as wide as he could, frowned a little, but dared make no further gesture of warning. If they opened fire, they might hit Edith, and once the plot was exposed, she would die with her father.

Vance's lips tightened for an instant. Selkirk had a slight hope that the man understood, might be playing a deep game to save the day, and once back in Brewster would expose the ruse where he could get aid. Though George Vance admired Edith

Voorhees, any jealousy Selkirk had felt toward Vance was overcome by his intense desire to see herself and her father safe, and, if possible, prevent this gigantic hoax.

Corellez was last to mount. Edith's face was still troubled as she reluctantly shook hands with Selkirk and followed Voorhees. Vance rode by the girl's side. A dozen of Corellez's men, pistols and rifles strapped on, went with the party.

Selkirk wanted to cry out, to shout a warning, but it would have been of no use. Death ringed him, and threatened Edith with the four or five heavily armed gunmen who lounged close by him.

The little party disappeared northward through the narrowing gap with its close stone ledges, the brush hiding the sight of them save for dust that rose from the horses' hoofs. A cold pall gripped Selkirk's fast beating heart.

The Voorhees party had not gone many miles when from the south rode a cavalcade of more armed men. They were led by Gila Mike Turner.

The scar-faced bandit at once took charge of the town, without any argument from Crole or the others. Now it was plain to Selkirk that the gunmen were hand-in-glove with Corellez and his hombres, just more of the same bunch. Gila Mike had simply formed a convenient front for any violence that had to be done.

Dr. Cassius Green was rigid with fright. "I'm — I'm not used to this sort of thing," he whined to Selkirk. "I can't stand it much longer, Selkirk."

"You've known all along that stuff was faked?" demanded Bert.

"Yes, all but a few pieces. The jewels are glass, colored imitations. The obsidian work is good but not Aztec. I was overcome, threatened with guns, they said I'd die if I didn't obey. You know what they did to Jackson!"

"Shut up!" growled a bandit guard, and shoved the frail Green roughly.

Gila Mike swung toward him, bow legs rustling with his heavy leather chaps. He approached Selkirk, glowered at him. Suddenly his huge hand flashed out, clapped Selkirk a mighty blow that made the young fellow's ear ring madly, half knocked him down.

Red rage blinded Selkirk. He came up on both feet and charged furiously at the giant outlaw. He managed to give Gila Mike a sharp punch in the nose; in return the bandit whipped out his six-gun, fired a shot that singed along Selkirk's battered ribs, staggering him. Sickness gripped the pit of Selkirk's stomach.

"The next bullet kills yuh," snarled Turner angrily. "I'm s'posed to hold yuh, but if yuh try that agin yuh die, savvy? I ain't takin' anything from a pilgrim skunk."

Selkirk and Green were seized, rebound. There was now no necessity to gag them and they were both tossed into the little hut near the path leading to Bald Top summit, behind which the sun was already dipping, shadowing the western edge of the deep gap.

The hours passed in torture to Selkirk. He could hear, from the direction of the Silver Steer, the sounds of increasing gaiety as Gila Mike and his bandits, freed of all restraint by the departure of the Voorhees party, whooped it up in celebration of success. While outside in the shadows, more of the great army of gunmen under Corellez and Turner stalked on night guard, bristling weapons ready.

Selkirk managed to sleep a little, cramped as he was. Each time he woke, he looked hopefully for the dawn through the chinks of the roughly built shack. But the tightness of the thongs kept disturbing him; Dr. Green uttered muffled sobs now and then, stirring fitfully, half dead from prostration

155

and fear.

On a box, a candle burned low on a scooped-out flat stone slab. The gunman who had been left, after supper, to watch the prisoners, leaned with his back against the wall, close to the door, within reach of his whiskey bottle from which he drank each time he awoke. The smell of the liquor was over-powering, and the man, a breed with swollen red eyes and a dark, evil face, was half stupefied by the alcoholic fumes.

The guard dozed from time to time, secure in the knowledge that his two charges were bound too efficiently to break loose. Besides, the clearing was swarming with his armed friends.

Lying along the base log that was set on the dirt to form the foundation for the shack, Bert Selkirk stewed in physical and mental agony. Then, suddenly behind him, he heard a faint sound. He listened. It came again. Something was at the rear. Making a picking noise, a sort of dull rustle.

"Selkirk!" a low whisper hailed him.

His heart leaped. "I'm here," he answered, turning his head to get as close as possible to the spot from which the voice came. Then a clot of adobe mud used in chinking was slowly shoved inward, and fell against his

ribs. Selkirk's eyes sought the chink. Someone was looking in at him from the rear of
the shack, he could make out the gleam of
an eye.

He realized who it must be: the man who
had saved him on Bald Top, from the
Apaches and Gila Mike. He had come at
last! Such was his confidence in Hatfield's
ability, he considered himself saved.

But then agony again seized him. What
could one man do against an army?

"Don't bother with me, get to Brewster
and save Voorhees. It's a cheat, the Aztec
treasure is faked!" he whispered rapidly.

"Sh— quiet," warned Hatfield.

The Ranger left the chink, knowing now
that Selkirk was inside and alive. In the
dense shadow afforded by the walls of the
hut, Jim Hatfield crept inch by inch around
the building.

With Don Ramon's Mexicans, armed to
the teeth, the Lone Wolf had made a swift
ride back to Corellez. Leaving his friends
down in the chaparral, he had come afoot
to the town, moving like a wraith through
the night. No one could compare with the
Ranger, not even the Apaches themselves,
at such work.

He had observed the thick array of guards
set about the clearing. A whole line had

been through the gap, blocking the way north.

Don Ramon knew all this country, told him that this was the direct, shortest route to Brewster. Other ways meant detours around precipices and high mountains, occupying several days. The canyon of death route where Don Luis had died, swung into the trail from Bald Top some miles south of Brewster. Don Luis had come that way for politic reasons.

After his first survey, Ranger Hatfield had returned to the south end of the gap. He had wanted some information and figured on how to get it.

Hidden in the brush, on the clearing's edge, the Lone Wolf had waited. To the left, he heard a stone roll under a sentry's boot. He had passed this fellow twice, once on his way in, again when he went out. The south end was not so well guarded as the constricted northern pass out of Corellez town.

The gunman carried a rifle. He also wore a pistol belt with cartridges. He paused to light a cigarette and the flare of the match showed his thin, whiskered face. The eyes were shifty and did not speak of much determination; he looked like a coward.

The Ranger made his decision swiftly. The

glow of the cigarette in the flaccid lips indicated exactly the position of the enemy. Hatfield sprang an instant later, and his long, slim but tremendously powerful hands closed on the gunman's scrawny throat.

All cries, save for a rattling gurgle, were cut off. The body wriggled on the neck like a chicken gripped in a man's hand. Then the Ranger had him down, knee on chest, holding him helpless, ramming the rat's bandanna into his mouth.

"Quiet, or I'll slit yuh wide open," he warned fiercely.

He lifted his prisoner and carried him quickly away. Don Ramon hissed to him two hundred yards along.

"Hold yore knife on him, Don," ordered Hatfield. "If he yells or tries to git away, cut out his gizzard." He was talking to terrify his captive, and he succeeded.

"Please, fer gawd's sakes, quit," gasped the rat, nerve entirely gone after feeling the might of the Ranger's grip.

"Talk, then. Tell me where's Corellez?"

"Gone to Brewster, with Voorhees and Vance, so help me!"

"For what?"

"I dunno, mister! They don't tell us nuthin', we work fer Gila Mike and that's all. We do what we're told!"

"I heard Mike whoopin' it up in the saloon. Where's that young feller Selkirk?"

The rat hesitated but the prick of Don Ramon's dagger loosened his tongue. "Tied up, with Green."

"Where?"

The rat had squeaked again. The Ranger left him in the hands of the Mexicans to be tied up and held, and crept, heading through the bush up the west, to reach the hut indicated by the prisoner Hatfield had taken.

Now, that he had made sure Selkirk was really in there, that the rat hadn't dared lie to him, Hatfield was going to get the East-erner out.

After speaking with Selkirk, and coming to the rear corner, the Ranger paused, for two men had stopped and were talking close to the front of the shack. Both were armed with rifles and pistols, but after a minute they swung on.

Hatfield crept stealthily around keeping well in the shadow cast by the building. He came to the little door, listened. Through the crack where the badly hung door did not fit in its frame, he saw the form of the guard, slumped in drunken stupor. With his hand, he pushed the door open an inch —

the sentry's eyes were closed. Hatfield saw that he was sound asleep.

The Lone Wolf quickly opened the door and slipped inside. He was on the guard as the latter's eye blinked wide, the scrape of the door having aroused him. The sharp crack of the Ranger's pistol against the guard's head stopped his cry, and his jaw dropped, chin touching his chest.

Hatfield hurried to Selkirk and slashed off his bonds. The young man rose unsteadily, needles and pins shooting through his limbs as the blood rushed back.

"Green! Get Dr. Green!" he gasped, as he limped about.

The Ranger went over and released the doctor. But the little man was unable to stand; he collapsed utterly. The Ranger picked him up and shouldered him.

"C'mon, let's sashay, Selkirk."

Bert Selkirk was the first outside, pushed by Hatfield. The Ranger came, carrying the limp form of the professor. As Hatfield stepped out, Selkirk staggering toward the nearby bush, a sharp cry of alarm sounded. Guns flashed off to their right, the guards had seen them.

Selkirk dived for the bush; Hatfield scurried after him. He felt Green give a convulsive jerk, and then the guns blared furiously, bullets whirling close about him.

"Git 'em, stop 'em!" a rough voice bawled. "Shoot 'em dead!"

CHAPTER XIII
THE BARRICADE OF DEATH

Hurrying feet, spitting rifles and revolvers, piercing yells filled the air. Gila Mike and his hombres dashed from the Silver Steer to join in the chase. The Ranger was handicapped by the weight on his back. He knew that the professor had been hit, and he could feel that he was no longer breathing. But it was a few minutes before he realized that Green was actually dead.

The Ranger discovered this in time to save himself for he would never have dropped Green had there been a spark of life in the unlucky doctor. The killers were almost upon him as he plunged into the bush, leaving the lifeless weight behind him. He whirled and began to shoot at the bunched men on his heels, the spitting of their slugs in the leaves close around him.

Selkirk blundered on ahead, calling back to him. The Ranger quickly overtook the young man, seized his wrist and they crashed through the rough, thorny growth, headed for the southern end of the gap.

Breath coming in heaving gasps from the terrific exertion, the two hurried to the spot where Don Ramon and his armed Mexicans awaited them. But more than a hundred gunmen were dashing after them, some about to cut them off from the Mexicans.

"Acosta — this way!" Hatfield's clear voice rang above the tumult.

A group of a dozen pursuers crashed into the bush a few yards ahead of them, others were rapidly coming up. The Ranger yanked Selkirk down behind a pile of jagged rocks, as a fusillade spattered about them. Hatfield began to shoot, coolly and carefully, to stop the rush and dampen the attackers' enthusiasm.

"Git 'em out! Tear 'em to pieces!" It was Gila Mike's roar, directing the battle.

Then there were sudden, sharp whoops from the south, and the swift-riding centaurs of Don Ramon Acosta, led by the slender hidalgo, swept up into the narrow valley.

"This way, Acosta!" shouted Hatfield again.

Ramon swerved his magnificent mustang, and was followed by his men. Their crossfire caught the bandits by surprise, and turned them into a wild retreat. Several crashed, screaming in death agony, under the concerted, fierce guns of the Mexicans.

Hatfield rose, six-shooter blaring as he charged out, completing the rout of the gunmen. Then Gila Mike managed to stop the stampede as more of his cohorts ran toward the center of the clearing. The dirt was thick with the gunmen, their fire making a roar like an army in battle.

With Ramon were forty Mexican vaqueros, peons mostly, but valiant men, all of them fighting for revenge. Obedient to the Ranger's orders, Acosta kept them back, and in a moment Selkirk and Hatfield were mounted, Goldy and spare ponies having been led up in the drag.

"We must get to Brewster quickly," gasped Selkirk, leaning sideward to speak to the Ranger. "Corellez has started there, he means to cash the check Voorhees has given him, a hundred and fifty thousand dollars for the fake treasure! We don't have much time."

"C'mon, charge 'em," shouted Hatfield, spurring Goldy into the van.

They hurled themselves at Gila Mike's line, a line of a hundred men spread across their path. The terrific gunfire rose in swelling crescendo, the yellow-red flashes lighting the immediate earth. Screams of wounded echoed in the gap, came back from the steep sides of the mountains in a maddened chorus.

Three of Don Ramon's Mexicans fell out of their saddles, struck by the tearing lead of Gila Mike's gunmen, lined up in a ragged front across their route. Then the swift ponies were in, smashing with hoofs and chests at the line, through which the riders' guns blasted holes. Men scattered from their path, intent only on saving their necks as the flashing, thousand-pound animals juggernauted into them.

"Mount and foller," shrieked Gila Mike, off to the side. "We got 'em now!"

Thirty-three of the Mexicans, Don Ramon, Hatfield and Selkirk, passed on through and headed north in the starry night. For three hundred yards they galloped on. The pursuit was organizing in Corellez, gunmen quickly mounting their ponies outside the Silver Steer.

"We shore ain't gittin' through easy as that," muttered Hatfield suspiciously. He had heard Gila Mike's cry as they cut the bandit line. He dragged on Goldy's rein.

"Watch it," he shouted warningly.

His keen eyes had seen the barricade ahead. The narrow trail was completely blocked. Two steep sides, thirty to forty feet high, hemmed in the trail, and across this ravine there was built of logs, rocks and brush a ten-foot high wall, a barricade of death.

As the horses slid to a stop in a cloud of dust, a blinding rifle fire began from the stockade. Two more Mexicans fell under it, and the Ranger felt the tear of a slug that cut a chunk of flesh from his forehead. Blood spurted into his eye as the bullet rapped the bone, and a lump like an egg rose immediately.

He fought for clarity of mind, as they turned. The pounding cohorts of Gila Mike were almost upon them. It was impossible to charge and climb that barricade, the only way out was back through the outlaw line again, or they would be trapped between two murderous fires.

The two parties, strung out, met head on. Fierce fighting ensued, pointblank shooting as men cursed and died in the hot hell of battle.

Then again they were in the clear, through the line of outlaws, firing back over their shoulders at Gila Mike and his henchmen. They had left thirty of the outlaws wounded or dying, but they had paid with plenty of their own blood.

Reforming again at the south end of the gap, Hatfield pushed Goldy close to Don Ramon, whose left arm was limp at his side, a bloody stain enlarging on his silken sleeve. The hidalgo was perfectly composed, no fear distorted his handsome face; Hatfield felt a surge of admiration for this blue-blooded Mexican.

"How long'll it take us to git round the other way?" the Ranger inquired.

Don Ramon shrugged. "Six, seven days, pairhaps. Better to go on foot but then we'd have no *caballos* on the other side!"

"That'd be too late," groaned Selkirk. "By that time Corellez'll have won, collected his money — !"

"We got to make it fast," agreed the Ranger, "if we're to save Voorhees. Tain't on'y the money." The clever Lone Wolf guessed what would occur, once the fortune was paid. In order to cover themselves from future prosecution, they must dispose of their victims forever.

Selkirk guessed the import of his statement. "Edith! They — they won't hurt her?"

The Ranger shrugged. "We got to git through quick," he repeated.

167

The outlaws had paused halfway down the gap, and were lining up. The Mexicans were in cover. Gila Mike's mob didn't relish a frontal attack on ambushed men. At a harsh call from Turner, they swung and cantered back past the Silver Steer.

"See? They're jest holdin' us. I callate that's orders," the Ranger observed. "We'll hafta fight to git to Brewster."

The Mexicans were breathing hard from the bloody fight. They rested, slouched in their saddles, smoking cigarettes, the red glow of the tobacco ends lighting their gleaming eyes.

"We're goin' out," Hatfield declared at last.

He swung, bending over the rat he had captured and who lay, bound up in the bush. The Ranger slashed his bonds. "Git up," he growled coldly.

The man was frightened. "Yuh — yuh ain't goin' to kill me, mister?"

"Not if yuh do as I tell yuh. A gang big as yores must have a password. Yore pals know yuh, don't they?"

"Shore. Why?"

"I'm givin' yuh a chanct. Ride up to that barricade and shout who yuh are, so they won't start lead rollin'; savvy?"

Hatfield stared up the gap. Dark forms of

bunched riders showed melting away north-ward. "On their way," he decided.

"What will you do?" inquired Don Ramon curiously. "We obey your orders, senor."

"Wait here, see what happens to me up there," the Ranger said. "If I don't come back, git to Brewster anyway yuh kin and give the alarm."

He mounted his prisoner on a horse. "Go ahaid, ride. "I'll be right behind yuh."

The rat's eyes gleamed. "Don't — don't shoot me in the back now."

"Ride!" said Hatfield his voice stern and forbidding.

The clearing in the gap where Corellez stood was almost free of Gila Mike's hombres. In the dark the Ranger rode behind his prisoner, and made good time to the barricade beyond. Now they were close on the heels of mounted gunmen.

A narrow gate stood open in the barricade, heavily armed men guarding it on the other side. The rat, half-hiding the slouched figure of the Ranger behind him; began to shout as he approached.

"One's Enough! One's Enough!" he said in a strained, unnatural voice. "Boys, don't shoot, it's Hank Murphy!"

Bristling guns covered the rat and the Ranger, who kept himself hidden as much as possible. As Murphy passed through the gate in the barricade, Hatfield spurred Goldy so the big sorrel leaped aside. Instantly shouts and shots rang out, as Murphy, safe now with his friends, shouted alarm.

A bandit leaped out, pistol spitting, and the Ranger flattened him with a lightning-quick shot. Then he was close in against the leafy barricade. He struck a match and touched it to the dry leaves. A little flame rose, and the Ranger started another blaze farther down, holding them back at the gate with well-placed bullets. By the time they realized what he was up to, the barricade was burning hotly and the smoke helped screen him from the gun-fighters. The smoke blew down on them and Hatfield swung, galloped back toward his friends.

The Lone Wolf was exhausted. He dismounted and threw the reins over Goldy's back.

"Keep a watch," he said to Acosta, "while I snatch forty winks. There's nothing to worry about till the barricade's finished burning. He lay down on the ground, was instantly asleep. It had been many hours since Jim Hatfield had been able to close his eyes.

When he woke, the dawn had come, the sky grey. The barricade had burned to the ground, the ashes were white and still smoking. Beyond, the exit to the north showed clear. Gila Mike had retreated, obviously a planned withdrawal.

The Ranger mounted Goldy and the party started north to Brewster. They rode swiftly through the warm, smoking ashes and charred sticks of what had been a mighty barricade.

Hatfield was in the lead, keen eyes traveling from side to side, watching for an ambush. A mile out of Corellez he noted the bush-masked ledges to the left, and pulled up.

"Wait here," he ordered. "I'll signal yuh."

He left Goldy with Don Ramon, and climbed up along the sloping hill, making his way from ledge to ledge till he was above the trail and could look down upon the scene. Men lay on their bellies on a lower ledge, a dozen of them, their horses hidden beyond in a screen of brush.

He opened fire upon them, taking careful aim. The hombre nearest him gave a convulsive leap, rolled off, into the trail below, his screech echoing in the confined space. The others swung, staring up toward the Lone

171

Wolf, training their guns on him.

Hatfield kept peppering them from cover, and after a few more of his accurate shots, they broke, knowing they were discovered, ran for their mounts and headed north. The Ranger returned to his party and they rode swiftly on. There was no time lost.

"If we keep them sidewinders in sight we'll know whether they got any more traps set," he said. "Callate it'll be tough gittin' into Brewster, though."

They rode through the rising sun and heat, pausing for nothing. He noted a camp site, evidently where the Voorhees party had stopped the first night out from Corellez. Hatfield figured they would travel slowly, with the middle-aged Voorhees and the young woman. But their pace had been Indian-swift and the cool of the evening found them forty miles to the north of Bald Top Mountain.

Throughout the day, now and then a distant glimpse had told Hatfield the outlaws he had driven from the ledge were riding hell-for-leather before them.

But the Mexes were weary, and Selkirk's face was drawn from exertion.

The young man made no complaint, but the Ranger could see he was about to drop.

Goldy still held his long stride and the Ranger's great frame could hold up longer than ordinary men. The short nap taken while the barricade burned had refreshed him enough so he had the power to shove on. But the pace grew slower and slower, as his companions dragged, keeping him back.

"Yuh better camp here," he said to Don Ramon. "Have a good guard set. I'm ridin' tonight. Meet yuh in Brewster."

He waited long enough for a bite of food from the Mexicans' saddlebags, some coffee and a smoke. Then, again warning Don Ramon to beware of ambushes, he remounted and headed northward. The Lone Wolf was once more on his solitary prowl.

The moon rose, lighting the way so he could easily follow it along. There was little dust in the air, but enough so he knew that the bandits were riding ahead of him. Just before dawn he entered the bush and slept for two hours. After hours of riding he was forced to rest Goldy and himself, for in the next few days he hoped to match his wits against the shrewdest gunmen of the Southwest.

The sunrise found him in the saddle; Goldy watered from a little stream that issued out of the mountains. The land descended rapidly now, countless draws and small hills breaking the bush. Through the warmth of noon he kept on and came to the split in the trail. When he had ridden south, he had swung east here and finally reached the canyon of death, where Luis, Don Ramon's brother, and his men had been wiped out so brutally, their valuables stolen from them for criminal purposes.

He drew up, staring at the site which showed that the Voorhees party had made a camp at this spot. Stirring the ashes of the fire with a stick, he found the dirt beneath still quite warm. They had been here the night before, their slower pace had allowed him to gain on them in spite of their long start. Nevertheless they would be in Brewster many hours before him.

Grimly, the tight chin strap of his Stetson accentuating the strong line of his rugged jaw, he swung once more into the steady pace that ate up the miles.

As he rode along he thought of the possibility of the fabulous sum for the fake treasure. In order to get actual money, cash a check given by Voorhees, it would be necessary for Corellez to wait until the bank opened at nine o'clock the following morning. Hatfield decided they would get to Brewster late that evening.

■ ■ ■ ■

The Ranger rode all afternoon and well into the night, and then he napped again while Goldy rested. In the first light of dawn, he was up. As he rode toward Brewster, he saw to the northeast high, rolling smoke in the sky. There was a big bush fire that way.

His eyes narrowed as he saw several birds winging it toward him. On the right was a huge, square granite boulder, and at one side freshly broken brush limbs where horsemen had smashed through.

There was a trail there and men were riding toward him. Hoofmarks told him that the outlaws he had flushed from the ledges north of Corellez had split into two groups here, half going into the bush, the rest keeping on to Brewster. He hurried around a bend, for his first object was to reach town and save Voorhees and his daughter.

A little after eight Hatfield trotted over the railroad tracks into Brewster. Down on the siding was Voorhees' private car. He trotted the travel-stained, lathered Goldy there. The car was deserted. He rode along the tracks and headed between the lines of houses, toward the central plaza.

Voorhees must be at the small hotel which

was an adjunct of the saloon. The bank would not open till nine o'clock and he thought he was in time to stop payment to Corellez.

The town was strangely quiet in the warmth of the yellow sun. On a porch he saw an old greybeard, leaning on his cane, lounging in a rocking-chair.

"Howdy," the Ranger said, drawing up. "Where's everybuddy, suh?"

"Gone out to fight the prairie fire," cackled the old fellow, "It's purty bad. Started last night and the wind's whippin' her in. Got to save the town."

A thick line corrugated the Ranger's forehead. Had that fire, then, been set deliberately by the outlaws to draw able-bodied men from the town? He believed it had. He crossed toward the hotel. As he neared the building, a line of armed men came out from either side, facing him.

CHAPTER XIV
BREWSTER!

They did not fire upon him, simply waited. Evidently they did not wish to alarm Dutch Voorhees by a pitched battle with this big deputy who had fought them so valiantly.

Hatfield hesitated. A gun-fight would

ordinarily bring Ex-Marshal Davis, now sheriff, and the men of Brewster, but they were gone to fight that fire. He judged the conflagration was about five or six miles northeast, sweeping down toward Brewster on the wind.

Quickly he turned the situation over in his mind. He could see that the door of Davis's office and jail was open. And there was a man inside, too, standing in the entry. It might be a deputy marshal.

The men surrounding the hotel were from Corellez, he could recognize many as fake excavators and hangers-on of the pasty-faced criminal. Others, he noted, were some of Gila Mike's outlaws. But he did not see the giant outlaw. He wondered where Turner was.

The bank, a square sturdily built structure of stone, was on the far side of the plaza. The Ranger, staying on the opposite side, ready to fight if interfered with, rode along the square. As he came close to the jail, more armed hombres came from behind the bank on the west side and blocked it from him. The men at the hotel lined up in the street, others showed at the north end beyond the lock-up, so that Hatfield was cut off entirely.

He might ride between buildings and

shoot his way through the closing circle. Goldy was weary; but he had taken a great deal of trouble to reach Brewster. The Ranger's long jaw set. With the townsmen away the outlaws had full charge of Brewster. And, Hatfield figured it would take an hour to ride to the fire and fetch Davis and help, another hour to get back. It was too close to nine A.M. to think of this.

Something quick and definite had to be done for by the time the posse returned, Corellez would have cashed Voorhees' check, and be on his way. He probably would take his victim with him and see that he died in the south hills, to protect himself from a dangerous witness to his crimes. Gila Mike, as usual, would make a good blind to hide behind, for the violence and murder that had occurred. The big bandit was on the dodge anyway, and was paid to shoulder all such blame.

The Ranger hesitated but an instant, then dismounted and slapped Goldy on the rump, sending the sorrel off to the side. If bullets flew, he didn't want the sorrel to catch any of them.

Then he saw them slowly closing in upon him. And though suspicious of a trap, there was nothing for him to do but step inside the jail.

■ ■ ■ ■

A smooth young man sat in the chair, facing him. The Ranger shut the door without taking his eyes off him.

"Howdy, depitty," the smooth fellow at the desk drawled.

"Howdy." Hatfield's slim powerful hands hung limp at his sides.

The man behind the desk wore a silver star set on a silver circle. The badge of Hatfield's famous organization, the Texas Rangers gleamed on his chest.

"I'm a Texas Ranger," the man went on fingering the badge. "Down here on a special mission."

Hatfield could not see his hands, below the desk. But he saw the slight twitch of the shoulder. He knew the man was an imposter, there to catch him off guard. That was why they had shooed him into the jail.

Jim Hatfield fell aside in a lightninglike movement, then his six-gun cleared leather and boomed in the small room. The faker's slug spattered on the adobe wall an inch from Hatfield's ear, but the Ranger's struck him in the head, ploughed along his scalp, parting his hair neatly. The young man tipped back violently in his chair, crashing on his back. He lay still, mouth gasping, like a fish out of water.

"Hey, Dude, did yuh git him?"

Hatfield whirled to face two more armed hombres who bounded from the cell room. He heard the scrape of their boots as they came at him, spitting curses of rage as they saw Dude was down.

The Ranger squatted behind the oak desk, and fired twice, in rapid succession. The first outlaw fell before he could get his gun trained on Hatfield, the second sent a shot that grooved the desk top and sang close over the Lone Wolf's head. Then the gunman joined his partner on the floor, drilled by a Ranger slug.

The Ranger leaped over to the entrance, threw the heavy bolt on the barred door that led into the street.

Hatfield's first act was to drag all three of his prisoners to an open cell, take their guns and bullet belts, and throw them in the lockup. Dude, the man with the Texas Ranger badge, was still unconscious, head lolling to the side. He was resting on the cheek, his tongue sprung between his teeth and blood clotted heavily in his hair.

"I'll be seein' yuh later, *amigo mio*," muttered Hatfield, long jaw set and neck corded.

"That star shore interests me in yuh!"

Warning sounds came to him and like a tiger he sprang out into the other room, pistol blaring at a man's head showing in the barred window. The rifle clanged on the bars, and the one outside, a hole blown through his forehead, sank down out of sight. His friends shattered the glass entirely but the bullets hit the ceiling.

The walls were of three foot adobe brick, and all the windows had heavy steel bars in them. The bolt was large and the door strong enough to withstand a hard attack.

Carefully Hatfield approached the window he had cleared, and peeked over the sill. A ticking clock on the shelf close by said nine o'clock.

Down the dusty street, lined with gunmen, the Ranger saw Dutch Voorhees come out of the hotel and step down from the low-built porch. Corellez walked with him, his pallid, death's head of a face turned toward the millionaire. Voorhees strolled slowly, listening to Corellez's words, sun gleaming on his thick spectacles, stout figure waddling from side to side. A couple more hombres, backers of Corellez, brought up the drag, eyes alert.

Corellez was steering Voorhees toward the bank, whose door was just opening. The porter hooked back the double entrance.

"Voorhees!" roared Hatfield. "Don't — !"

His words were drowned out and he was forced to duck as bullets spanged into the walls, some through the window, close past his head.

Dutch Voorhees hesitated, staring at the jail. He asked a question and Corellez said something to him, but they walked on.

The Ranger pulled a chair over, set it at an angle away from the window. From this vantage point he could look out and command the bank's front door. His was safe in this spot for in order to hit him from the plaza the outlaws would have to make a lucky shot or else come right up to the window and poke their guns through the bars.

He had plenty of ammunition and guns, including the .45 shells in the belts he had taken off the three who had tried to drygulch him. He placed a shot that spurted dust up in front of Voorhees. Corellez was on the other side of the old man, protected by Voorhees' body. Dutch stopped, turned and started to retreat; he did not fancy being under fire.

The success of this play, amused Hatfield. He intended to keep the rich man out of the bank as long as possible. The Ranger sent slugs that cut the face of the bank's front door and also spattered the ground between Voorhees and the entrance. Corellez, gripping Voorhees' arm, suddenly turned, and ran back out of sight.

"Now what?" muttered Hatfield.

Jim Hatfield tried to follow the moves of Corellez and his victim, but they did not appear for some minutes. When he next saw them, they were crossing the road way down toward the tracks, out of six-gun range. He glimpsed them once again as they crossed the gap between two houses on the bank side of the road.

Then the Ranger saw through Corellez's plan. He was escorting Voorhees inside the bank and collecting his money, having entered by a rear door.

"A good idee," he decided.

If he could, himself, get over to the other side of the road without being shot down, he might make the bank on the plaza. Inside its strong walls he could defend himself, hold them off for hours, prevent Corellez from winning his objective, which was to obtain a fortune in cash from the deceived Voorhees.

But the road was swarming with outlaws, gunmen ordered to kill him on sight.

The little town, lazy under the balzing sun, seemed quite peaceful. The odor of burnt grass and wood drifted down on the breeze, the air hazy. Wispy white clouds floated in a turquoise sky. Saddle horses dozed in the shade cast by wooden sidewalk awnings, awaiting their bandit masters.

He must get to the bank. But, as he opened the thick jail door a few inches, that space was immediately covered by hot lead that forced him to leap back, and slam it shut. To die now meant failure and the triumph of his foes.

The big Ranger strode back to the rear of the square front jail room to get the six-shooters he had taken from his prisoners. Through the open door that led into the space where the barred cells were, he heard in the lull of comparative quiet the delirious moaning of Dude, the smooth hombre who had tried to catch him by posing as a Ranger.

"That's the way they got Gila Mike outa here," he mused. "On'y mistake they made was figgerin' I was a depitty sheriff, never guessin' I was a Ranger, down here to find Martin's murderer."

Hatfield was keenly interested in the man who'd had that distinctive badge. He had purposely creased him, to preserve him for future questioning. He should know a lot about Ranger Martin's end. He strode to the cell.

"Don't — don't let that big galoot git me, Boss — don't let him!" whined Dude.

The Ranger went into the cell, stooped beside the young man. The drying blood showed in his hair, face twisted, eyes rolling as he mumbled words the Ranger could not make out. Hatfield took hold of his shoulders, lifting him, shaking him.

"Who was it finished off Ranger Martin?" he asked in the fellow's ear.

Dude was delirious from his head injury and he was mumbling thickly.

"That yuh, Boss?" he asked. "Huh — what yuh — what yuh want? Corellez says everything's okay, claims yuh'll win. I gotta hand it to yuh, Boss!"

Hatfield's tanned, rugged face grew puzzled. Fresh interest glowed in his grey-green eyes. The prisoner was off his head from the effects of the bullet the Ranger had clipped him with, but he might well speak the truth in such a state.

"Corellez, ain't he the boss?" he demanded.

The man gave a silly laugh. "Aw, quit yore foolin', Boss."

The boss! Then it wasn't Corellez. Could it be Gila Mike? Not likely; he was another front, the strong arm killer for the men higher up. Was it that mysterious person whom Hatfield had actually spoken with through the communicating pipe in Bald Top Mountain?

Hatfield shook him again. But as he prepared to draw out his important information, the ground began to tremble, raucous bellowings rose from outside.

"Yipee! Head off that leader, Frankie — they're rushin' the town!"

Hatfield ran out, slamming the self-locking door again. From the window, as the heavy beatings of the earth grew in deafening volume, he saw the forms of steers that broke in bunches across Main Street and the plaza, dashing wildly in and out between houses. The dust they raised rapidly increased until it blotted out everything but the space a few yards about him. Ponies that had been quietly standing a moment before, broke loose and ran in the rush.

The Ranger saw that a herd was on a stampede, had run into the town. The flashing shapes of riders trying to get them under control, he glimpsed as he watched. Yells, bellows, thudding of hoofs, mingled together in the clouds of white dust.

"My chance," he muttered, and, grabbing up spare guns, he threw a couple of belts over his broad shoulders and leaped again to the front exit. He slid back the steel bolts and flung the door wide open. He was on his way out.

Chapter XV
The Bank

Through drifting dust the cows ran, blindly charging this way and that. Hatfield glimpsed the foot-high brand on an animal that rushed past the door — ME Connected. Milton English and his men must be riding along with these locoed critters. The dust blew into his face, sifting in his eyes.

"Wind's shiftin'," he growled. That meant the fire would blow away from Brewster, and the fighters there could come back to town, for it would die out across its own burned areas, backfired by its own destruction.

The thousand-pound, sharp-horned steers were very dangerous to a man afoot; reddened eyes and flaring nostrils, tails up, showed their excited state. But Hatfield was glad of the chance they gave him.

He jumped out into the open and started

across the road, a six-gun clenched in either hand. A dozen men waited up on porches right across the wide plaza. The instant they glimpsed his tall, swift-moving form in the dust, a shout went up, and they began to fire but he opened up on them with both guns, bullets burning with deadly accuracy along the line.

A shriek of anguish mingled with the other sounds. The Ranger was halfway across when a big bull that dashed close to him received several slugs designed for Hatfield and went crashing in the dirt. The Ranger leaped over the twitching body and, blasting with his pistols, headed straight for the space between two buildings which he had cleared with his fire and the help of the charging steers.

Two big critters came up behind him as the vultures of Corellez and Gila Mike ran to the house corner in an attempt to shoot him in the back. He leaped sideward to escape the rushing charge of the beast on the left, and was brushed by its barrel ribs and spun against the side of the building. He recovered himself, but the bullets that followed him now were blind as he faded into the dust cloud.

Guns out, ready, their muzzles flaring at angles to cover his front, he turned and ran head-on into two armed men who split before his rush. Their slugs ripped through his clothes, one biting the flesh of his thigh. Torn by the terrible sting of it, Hatfield shot pointblank into one's belly and swept the other back with a hard jab to the eye with the sharp barrel of his second gun.

A heavy-set man on a white mustang, mouth and nose covered by his bandanna, swept up.

"What the hell's goin' on here?" he roared furiously. "Quit that shootin', yuh fool, yuh'll turn 'em back into town agin!"

"English!" growled Hatfield.

Milton English, boss of the ME Connected, stared at the Ranger for instants before recognizing him.

"Why, it's that salty depitty!" he cried.

"Git yore men and bring 'em to the bank, pronto!" ordered the Lone Wolf.

"Holdup?" English asked, as he jerked his rein, already obeying the Ranger's command.

"Worse!" Hatfield let it go at that, no time to explain. He was running for the back door of the stone bank.

An outlaw there ordered him to halt. The Ranger put him out of the way with a bullet that smashed his arm, knocked him aside and went in.

Great chest heaving, he looked quickly about him. He was in a small rear entry, empty of men. He slammed the back door, locked it behind him, started up front.

There were side rooms where clerks worked at desks over ledgers and accounts. The public part of the Brewster Bank ran between two long counters behind which tellers stood. Only two citizens were inside, drawing or depositing; most everybody was out fire-fighting.

Hatfield saw a glass-paneled door marked *John Todd, President.* It was shut. Two men he recognized as outlaws from Corellez stood guard before it. They suddenly spotted the Ranger as he came at them.

"Back," Hatfield snapped, smoking six-guns aimed.

Before the level iciness of those eyes they dared not risk a gun-fight with him at such close quarters. They had been in Corellez's saloon when he had bucked the gang that evening, knew his fighting ability.

They backed off, staring at him with hands raised as he commanded. The Ranger turned the doorknob and was inside, slamming it behind him, stepping along the wall away from the frosted glass to protect his back.

Three men sat at the large desk. Voorhees, side toward the door, Corellez opposite him; and facing Hatfield directly was John Todd, the elderly president of the Brewster Bank. On the flat top of the desk were high piles of currency.

The Ranger, face stained with powder smoke and dirt, blood trickling from his racked body, clothing ripped from bullets and thorns, remained poised inside the door. For an instant, he stood regaining his breath after his swift dash.

Corellez turned his pallid face and his eyes grew round as icy moons. John Todd was frowning at the battered Hatfield who stood there with guns drawn and ready.

"Bandits — holdup!" gasped Corellez.

The bank president swiftly dropped his hand toward the open drawer under his elbows.

"Leave yore gun lay," ordered Ranger Hatfield. "Reach!"

There was an alarmed frown on Voorhees' heavy, seamed face. He had not recognized Hatfield.

"Yuh can't get away with this," declared Todd hotly. He was an old-time cattleman and believed in direct action. But the steady gleam in the Ranger's grey-green eyes, the relentless, long-barreled Colts that had him covered cold, made his hands rise; a man had to do as ordered till he got a chance to make his play.

Corellez, seizing the instant Hatfield had to take to protect himself from the alarmed president, slid from his seat to the floor, down behind the desk. He fired on Hatfield just as the Ranger started to shift to a spot where he could keep a direct bead on Corellez.

Hatfield felt the whirl of the bullet an inch fraction from his ear. It spun by and thudded into the wall.

All Hatfield could see of Corellez was the man's legs; he crouched, sent a bullet along the floor. Corellez yipped in agony, as the slug ripped through his boot and smashed his ankle. His next bullets were wild as his hand spasmodically jerked from the pain.

"Hey, Corellez — what's up?" Someone banged on the door with the butt of a gun.

"First man inside dies," the Ranger roared and swung to put one through the glass as a warning.

Corellez, froth on his lips, was cursing as he rolled in frenzy. He tried again to shoot at Hatfield but the Ranger drilled him through the collarbone. Corellez straightened out on his back, writhing on the floor.

Hatfield stepped over, kicked the gun from the relaxed hand, watching the others. Todd again made an attempt to get his gun from the drawer.

"I ain't shootin' yuh or robbin' anybody," Hatfield said gravely. "I come to purvent sech. Voorhees, whatever yuh do, don't give out any money! That Aztec stuff is mostly fake. Corellez and his pals are cheatin' yuh."

"Eh? Vot is dat?" demanded Voorhees, scowling. "I don't understand. I recognize you now, you're the fellow who made so much fuss in the south. Corellez says you're really a bandit posing as an officer —"

There were confused shouts and some shooting in the corridor. Then the door suddenly opened. Milton English, cocked pistol in hand, stuck his in. A couple of his riders were right behind him.

"We chased 'em outa the bank," he cried. "But the town's lousy with 'em, Depitty. However, the wind's shifted and soon everybody'll be back. Me'n the boys were tryin' to turn our herd east; that fire made them start for California!"

"Yuh know this big hombre, Milt?" growled President Todd. "Is he a bandit?"

"Shucks, no," English replied with a hearty guffaw. "Davis done made him a depitty. He's a right salty hombre and okay as they come. I'll ride the river with him any time!"

The president emitted a sigh of relief. "That's good. I shore thought we was in for trouble, Milt."

"Den vot he says iss true; I vas being hoaxed?" demanded Voorhees. "Vot about Professor Green, and Selkirk, and Vance; dey all declared the pieces Corellez offers are authentic?"

"They was forced to," explained Hatfield. "Green's murdered, Corellez's men tried to finish Selkirk. Vance they fooled, he's no expert. They done put Prof. Jackson in bed for a month, yuh remember —"

"But I've got to see Mr. Voorhees — at once!" An excited voice protested from the corridor.

Some heavier shooting sounded distantly outside, but quickly died away. Another ME Connected puncher came to the door, reported to English.

"Sheriff's back, Boss," he told the rugged cowman. "We're chasin' them galoots outa town!"

One of the cowboys who stood guard outside stepped in too. "A man named Vance here says he's gotta come in," he said distrustfully. "Shall I let him?"

"Shore," Hatfield answered.

George Vance, face drawn and pale, eyes frightened, ran into the room.

"Mister Voorhees, Gila Mike's kidnapped Edith! It's horrible. They left this note —"

Voorhees cursed. His ruddy face paled. "I vant to see," he muttered, his hand held out.

Hatfield saw the crude scrawl on the dirty sheet of paper as Voorhees, hands trembling, held it before his near-sighted eyes.

"Send fifty thousand or yer dauter dyes," the Ranger read. "No sheriffs, savvy, and ony one man to bring it. Gila Mike Turner."

"They must have taken her during the night, right out of her hotel room," Vance said miserably. "When the shooting began a while ago I hustled up to make sure she'd stay in and not get hurt by a stray bullet. When she failed to answer my knocking and calls, I finally opened the door and found the note on her pillow, pinned there with a knife. She hadn't slept in her bed."

"Ve must ged her back at once!" Voorhees cried pounding the desk. "I'll pay, pay anyt'ing. Yess, I haff the money all ready, too, the money I meant to giff Corellez for the Aztec treasure. Hurry, hurry, we mus' safe Edith!"

Hatfield did not blame the father for his

reaction. Voorhees was willing to pay over any sum to Gila Mike for the safe return of his daughter.

"George!" shrieked Corellez. "George!"

Vance turned, saw the bloody figure on the floor behind the desk.

"Corellez — what's happened to him?" he gasped, stepping over to stare down at the twitching, deathly face.

"He's a crook and murderer, Vance," Voorhees growled. "He made monkeys oud of us."

Hatfield touched Milton English's elbow. "Come outside a sec, will yuh?" he asked in a low voice.

In the corridor he said hurriedly, "I'll be right back. Keep 'em all inside, savvy, don't let anybody out."

"Okay," the ranch owner replied.

The bandits had mounted and rapidly ridden out of Brewster as the townspeople began to come in from the dying fire. The air was clearer, the shifting wind had blown back the smoke pall and the dust was settling after the stampede of the steers of the ME Connected.

Hatfield headed swiftly toward the jail, long strides covering the distance. Sheriff Davis was just dismounting at the door.

"Why, howdy!" he cried, seeing the Ranger. "What's happened to yuh? I bin wonderin' where yuh was, Hatfield."

"Come inside," Hatfield said. "I got a job to do, Sheriff."

The two entered the jail and headed for the cells. Dude, the smooth hombre, lay on his back, staring up at the ceiling. He was still groggy. The Ranger carried him out into the office and placed him on the floor.

"By heaven," cried Davis, "that's the sidewinder that took Gila Mike outa here!"

"Got whiskey?" Hatfield asked the sheriff.

Davis produced a pint flask of red liquor, and the Ranger poured a stiff drink down Dude's throat. The stimulant soon took effect and Dude, weak through he was, looked up into the rugged face of his nemesis.

"Yuh made a little error, Dude," drawled Hatfield. "I happen to be a member of the Texas Rangers so I knowed yuh was lyin'. My name's Jim Hatfield."

"The Lone Wolf!" gasped Dude, who had heard of this big officer as the biggest threat to gunmen above the Rio Grande.

"Yeah, the game's up. Yore gang's busted, Corellez shot, the rest on the run. Yuh murdered Ranger Martin. That was his star yuh had. Yuh'll swing fer that!" Hatfield's eyes were wide with anger and his voice sharp with revenge.

"No, I didn't kill him!" cried Dude. "The boss done it!"

"Who's yore boss? C'mon now, talk. I ain't foolin'!"

Dude knew he was through. He was plainly afraid of the mighty Lone Wolf. He started to talk, words gushing a confession from his lips.

"The boss stabbed him —" he began.

Chapter XVI
Ransom!

Twenty minutes later Hatfield, Sheriff Davis at his spurs, hustled back to the president's room in the Brewster bank. The Ranger entered first. His grave eyes, alert as he paused inside, darkened as he looked around the president's office.

Voorhees was pacing up and down, deep wrinkles of anguish in his face, near-sighted eyes blinking with nervousness and worry.

"Edith — my girl!" he muttered.

Corellez still lay on the floor, moaning. The president and English were smoking cigars, blue tobacco smoke rolling to the white ceiling.

"Where's Vance?" Hatfield demanded.

"He's gone to pay that ransom and bring

back Edith," replied Voorhees.

"Yuh let him go?" the Ranger said to English.

"Shore, I didn't think yuh included him," the ME boss replied. "Voorhees here couldn't wait to start him on his way and I don't blame him. No tellin' what that murderous Gila Mike'll do if he's balked. Best way is to save the gal and then go out after Turner."

"So yuh handed Vance fifty thousand dollars!"

"Surely. He vent off to safe Edith," Voorhees answered. "She vorth everyt'ing I haff! Vance loves her; he vanted to marry her, I know. He hass been a great help."

"He's one cunnin' rascal," muttered the Ranger. The grim lines of his mouth tightened as he started for the door. Vance had pulled the wool over everybody's eyes.

Sheriff Davis was more talkative about it. "Why, yuh danged fool," he yelled, "Vance is the boss of the hull crooked shebang! We just wormed it outa Dude, a delirious bandit lieutenant, the Ranger clipped and locked up in the jail. Dude posed as a Ranger to save Gila Mike; we got the hull story.

"Corellez was Vance's front, and Gila Mike's dirty work man for the gang. It was all Vance's idea, to cheat Voorhees by sellin' him that junk!"

"Ranger, did yuh say this salty depitty's a Texas Ranger?" cried Milton English.

John Todd, the bank president, was impressed, too.

"Shore he is! That's Jim Hatfield, the best officer they got. Cap'n McDowell sent him down to see 'bout the murder of Ranger Martin and the rustlin' of yore stock, Milt."

"No dang wonder he kin fight like he was an army," English exclaimed. "Say, shake agin, Ranger Hatfield. I've heard of yuh — the Lone Wolf, huh! It's a pleasure, mister."

"Me, too," Todd chimed in. "The place is yores, Hatfield."

Hatfield paused at the door, face grave. "Organize yore pursuit, Davis. I'll be ridin' on Vance's trail. What Davis says is true. Vance planned this hull business. Him havin' worked for Voorhees before as a field man, he knowed jest what Voorhees'd fall for. He had seen that stuff the Acostas had. He killed the Mexicans and took their goods and he put in some junk of his own he'd run acrost. He hid hisself so well this is the fust hint we got of his connection with the thieves."

"But — but don't let dem hurt Edith,"

begged Voorhees. "She's vorth everyt'ing!"

Hatfield nodded. "I'll git her back," he promised, and was gone.

The Ranger hurried to find Goldy. The sorrel had strayed off, out of the dense dust and smoke, but whistles brought him trotting to Hatfield's side. The Ranger mounted and rode to the little hotel across the plaza.

Edith Voorhees was not in her room. Vance, the arch criminal, had told the truth so far; her bed was undisturbed. There was even a knife blade rent in the pillow and the dagger lay on the floor.

"I s'pose he was still hopin' he could fool us," mused Hatfield, "and stay clear outwardly."

Guns reloaded, a drink under his belt, he returned to the road and mounted the golden sorrel. Vance had been seen, heading south across the railroad tracks. But he had a two-mile start, and the Ranger knew he would have taken the best of horses to make good his escape.

Hatfield was out of sight, well on his way, before Sheriff Davis, heading a large posse, took up the chase. The south trail showed greatly cut up; it was plain that the bandits had all retreated this way, leaving many dead and wounded in Brewster.

Dust still hung in the warm air, dust risen

from the hoofs of the killers' mounts, running this way hell-for-leather since the jig was up. The Ranger knew his first task was to rescue Edith Voorhees from the hands of the outlaws; that Gila Mike actually had her, he had no doubt.

This would explain Gila Mike's hurrying north from Corellez, so as to be on hand near Brewster in case Vance needed him. The deadly, but coldly logical brain of George Vance had figured on every possibility; he had planned for all contingencies. No doubt he had held this kidnaping business in reserve, in case he must have a way to bargain with Voorhees.

"And if he'd sold that there Mexican stuff to Voorhees, why he could've purtended to rescue her from the outlaws," he told Goldy. The sorrel's ears twitched and he bobbed his head as though he savvied what the big man he loved was saying. "Mebbe he hoped to be her hero, at that, and marry her. Then have Gila Mike kill her old man and she gits all the cash there is in the world, fer Vance, inherits it from her dad.

"Shore, I wouldn't put it past him at all, Goldy. As I said, he's one cunnin' rascal. The smartest we ever trailed. We shore come close to growin' donkey ears this trip, thanks to him. Now we *gotta* ketch up with him."

The Ranger rode fast, simply watching for signs along the sides. The many hoofs that had passed along the main trail hopelessly confused it, and he did not attempt to pick out Vance's tracks.

He had a hunch as to where Edith Voorhees might be held hostage. He did not forget how half of the bandits who had ridden ahead of him, up from Corellez, had branched off a few miles below Brewster, branched off eastward at the square boulder. Gila Mike would be lying over there in the chaparral, so that Vance could easily get in touch with him.

As usual, when he rode, he kept an eye on the sky ahead. White puffs of clouds sailed across the light blue of the heavens. He hoped the weather kept warm, fair.

He was nearing the square granite boulder which he had decided marked the trail into Gila Mike's temporary camp in the chaparral a short way outside the cowtown. It was here he had noted the tracks, the startled, flying birds that told him men were in there.

A low hail came to him and his long hand dropped toward his six-gun. He drew rein, staring at the pale-faced man who rose from

203

out of the brush from the right margin of the way.

It was Don Ramon Acosta.

"Senor Americano, amigo mio," Acosta cried, "So glad I am to see you!" His voice held a queer anguished note.

"Where's Selkirk and yore men?" demanded Hatfield tersely.

There was dried blood on the Mexican hidalgo's lean, proud face. His expensive clothing was dirty, ripped badly.

"Selkirk ees dead," replied Don Ramon sadly.

A pall of gloom fell on the Ranger's stout heart. He had liked the young easterner and had found him a brave man. In addition, he knew what sadness this would bring to Edith Voorhees.

"Ees good to see you, *amigo*," Acosta continued. "Not so long after you left, Gila Mike and a band of hees hombres fell on us and we had a terrible battle below here. Selkirk was shot down, hees pony riddled. He never move' after he heet the groun'. They drove us back into the bush and not till night came could we make our escape, those left of us. I went to fin' Selkirk's body but they had drag' heem off. I could see the path hees corpse made in the sand. We had to rest.

"Finally we caught our horses and start' north once more. A short while ago we heard men coming. There was only a handful of us lef' and we were short of ammunition, and couldn't chance another fight, so we hide up on the slope. More and more pass', outlaws of Gila Mike and thees Corellez."

"Did yuh see a slim sidewinder with a dude's outfit, and little black mustache?"

"*Si, si.* Señor Vance, you mean."

Hatfield started. "Yuh know him?"

"Oh, *si,* yes. Some weeks ago he veeseet our home, in Mexico, was when Luis still live'. Eet was Vance advise' Luis he should take hees goods to sell in the United States. When Luis weeshed *mucho dinero* to pay the debt of our town and help our peons, he collect' what we had made with such pains, and the old models Vance so admire', and start' north. Vance told heem to take the canyon route, said the United States would charge us great moneys to bring such goods in; also, Mexico has an export duty on silver."

Hatfield shook his head. "Yeah, he's one hell of a cunnin' rascal," he muttered. "He shore planned it out fine. Had a spy watchin' for that smuggler train to start, and got the rest of the set-up ready!"

■ ■ ■ ■

The whole picture was clear now.

The Mexicans of the Acosta village, the sleepy little town in the hills beyond the Rio Grande, had made with great skill and pains copies of the few Aztec relics that had been passed down from generation to generation in the Acosta family. They had also contributed their own fine work in pottery and carvings. They had put their trademark on the bottom of the bowls.

When Hatfield had rubbed off the dust and grime which Vance's men had applied to make the objects appear antique, he had seen that mark, which Don Ramon had said was placed on the village products. These Vance had ruthlessly stolen for his murderous plans.

"Yore stuff oughta still be up in them caves, yuh kin git it. If yuh want money, yuh kin sell the few pieces that are real to Voorhees for a good sum, yore silver, too. That Vance hombre, he's head of the whole shebang; I don't doubt he finished yore brother, him and his killers."

Acosta gasped. "I — I never guess'! By the Virgin, you mus' be right, señor I see eet now. Why, I even tried to get down and stop heem when he rode by an hour ago, to warn heem of the outlaws I have seen! But he was riding swiftly, and more of our enemies were coming."

Don Ramon stared down the trail, in the direction George Vance had ridden. His brown hands were tightly clenched and his teeth ground together.

"I understan'," he repeated.

"Did yuh see Gila Mike ride through that east trail, with a young lady pris'ner?" asked the Ranger.

Acosta shook his head. "No."

"Might've gone through in the dark, though. I'm chancin' it. Got to, it is the on'y place she could be. Yuh wait here and swing some of the sheriff's men thisaway. Tell the others to haid south after bandits and Vance. They getter git to Corellez and clean it out."

Don Ramon nodded as Hatfield swung Goldy toward the east, past the square granite rock. The trail was very narrow, thorny branches reaching to switch Goldy as the big horse pushed through. The land mounted slowly, rocks protruding here and there.

He rode for half an hour, in and out of the chaparral. His keen eyes sought for signs; he could tell that, though this was not a much used trail, many men had ridden it in the past day or two.

He paused under a tree that shaded and concealed him from the heights he saw ahead. There were some reddish cliffs that broke the country a few hundred yards beyond. The sun flashed from something metallic that way. He dismounted, led Goldy back out of sight, hitched the sorrel's rein to a bush low enough so the golden horse could nip the grass at his hoofs. Then he started silently along the trail, pausing now and again to listen.

He went very carefully as he neared the point where he'd seen that flash. There were two big rocks between which the horse track passed. The Ranger crouched off the way, waiting. Finally a bandit showed on one side, appearing from behind a rock. He rested his rifle on the stone as he peered down the trail toward the hidden Hatfield; evidently he had heard something, perhaps Goldy's hoof scraping on a stone, for he was listening intently and frowning.

Hatfield began a slow stalk to work around behind him. No Indian ever moved with such skillful stealth as the big Ranger. The gleam of the sun on that rifle barrel had warned him of the guard; and he guessed

Gila Mike's camp would be near at hand, probably up on those overhanging ledges which would be an ideal spot.

It took him several minutes to reach a point where he could see along the rear side of the rock. From there he could cover the outlaw sentry.

He picked up a round stone, tossed it into the air, so it rolled in the trail. The guard was instantly alert, rifle grasped in both hands, watching down the path, just sombrero and eyes showing over his rock.

But he grew impatient after a minute, and emerged. He tiptoed slowly along the trail, pausing now and again to listen and look, rifle ready before him.

The Ranger leaped when the guard came abreast of him. His strong fingers clasped the gunman's throat, throttled all outcry, as he bore him to the hard earth. A sharp blow from his fist knocked the bandit unconscious, and then Hatfield hurried on toward the ledges, leaving the sentry as he lay.

There was a corral below built of poles and uprights; in it many ponies. Up on the slope he saw the camp, men lounging on the shady side of the hill.

He cut around through the bush, keeping low, and went on past the camp. Cautiously he started for a sharp-angled turn. He straightened up as he came out on a narrow ledge a few yards over the camp.

Fifteen feet from him stood Gila Mike Turner. The giant bandit's hard face had puzzled lines in it. Turner had heard something that alarmed him, for he was facing Hatfield, arms limply hanging at his sides.

The eyes of the two men met full as they faced one another.

CHAPTER XVII
GIANTS DUEL

"Reach fer the sky —" began the Ranger.

But before the words were out of his mouth, Gila Mike Turner began his lightninglike draw. His great hand traveled with the speed of light to the smooth stock of his six-shooter. He drew the weapon, thumb joint on hammer sput, the pistol cocking by its own weight as it came up into firing position, nose seeking the Ranger's vitals.

Hatfield and Gila Mike had started about even, though the lawman had given the outlaw a chance to surrender without a fight, in the tradition of Western law. But no one had ever equaled the Ranger on the draw-and-fire.

The skill of the Ranger's long, thin hand, icily steady nerves, the lion heart within him, combined with a keen-edged brain to make him the most dangerous of antagonists in such a duel. Only instant fractions were taken up by actions of the antagonists.

Gila Mike's gun boomed and Hatfield staggered, teetering on his spread feet. But the Ranger's pistol had spoken the shade of a second ahead of Turner's and that had been enough to prevent the outlaw's gun muzzle from rising high enough to kill the Lone Wolf.

The giant outlaw's slug had torn a chunk of flesh from Hatfield's left leg, six inches above the knee. But the Ranger's bullet had buried itself deep in Gila Mike's brain.

The barrel-chested giant, his murderous, deadly career blasted by the Ranger's gun, stood on his boots for a moment. The whole bridge of his flat nose was smashed in by the bullet, and blood spurted from it in torrents as, impelled by his last conscious movement, Gila Mike tumbled over on his face and lay still.

Yells of fury warned Hatfield that Gila Mike's followers had heard the shots, and had seen him destroy their leader. He limped, left leg stiffening rapidly, for the corner of rock, as they began shooting up at him, spattering on the face of the cliff with slugs.

He held them off for minutes, steady guns driving them to take shelter as they could. They were losing their first hot-headed desire to tear him to pieces for killing Gila Mike, and were planning a way to work around above him and smoke him out. Then yells from the trail announced that Sheriff Cal Davis and his hastily recruited posse-men were rushing in, swung this way by Don Ramon, according to Hatfield's instructions.

Protected by the redstone bulge of the cliff rock, the Lone Wolf contented himself with sending a nasty enfilading fire down at those outlaws who tried to stand against Davis's party. His heavy .45 slugs sent sprawling two bandits who tried to rally their friends.

As the leaders crumpled the others broke, running helter-skelter for the bushy mesquite and huisache ridges. Some retreated, dashing within a hundred feet of Hatfield, whose deadly pistols boomed over and over, slashing all resistance, panicking the bandits.

With whoops of victory, Davis led his fighters on the bandit camp, seizing prisoners, smashing down opposition. As the affair degenerated into a rout of the outlaws, Hatfield stepped out on the ledge, glancing briefly at Gila Mike, stiffened in death on the broken shale.

Up a hundred yards past Turner, he heard the cry of a woman. Leaping over the dead bandit chief, he saw a brown tarpaulin stretched across a deep, triangular cleft in the cliff face. Two men who had been there were trying to climb like mountain goats up the cliff from notch to notch; they had evidently been guarding someone.

"Help!" cried Edith Voorhees. She came out, arms raised high, signaling to the sheriff below. Her face was pale and drawn, but she did not seem to be harmed.

Hatfield hastened toward her as fast as his wounded leg allowed. A rifle bullet from below spanged up, hit on the cliff, striking near one of the climbing men, he lost his hold and plunged, body sprawled in the air. His cry thudded out from his lungs as he landed on his back and lay still.

An over-enthusiastic posseman who did not recognize Hatfield fired at him. The Lone Wolf called to Sheriff Davis, who immediately gave hurried orders to his men and started up to join the Ranger. Edith, turning, saw Hatfield's grim, bloody figure as he limped toward her. She shrank back out of sight in the cleft, evidently afraid of him, not knowing who he was.

Approaching, he found her sitting on a

flat rock, her body shielding a prostrate figure wrapped in blankets. Hatfield's eyes widened as he recognized the drawn face of Bert Selkirk, a red-stained bandage around his head, face drained of blood, eyes closed.

"I'm a friend, ma'am," the Ranger told her quietly. "Is Selkirk alive?"

"Yes, yes. But he needs attention. The bullet that hit him nearly struck his brain, but he's not dead, I've nursed him as well as I could. We've been held prisoner. They said they'd keep Selkirk and that'd make me do anything they wanted." Her gaze fell before the steady eyes of the Ranger, and her cheeks flushed. Her affection for Selkirk was plain.

He knelt beside Selkirk, felt his pulse, observed his color and breathing. He nodded.

"Yuh're right, ma'am. He'll pull through, shore enough."

She gave him a grateful look, as Hatfield silently turned away.

"Where are you going?" she inquired.

"After George Vance," he said quietly.

"George? What's he done?"

"He's the one's caused all yore trouble, ma'am. That Aztec stuff was a fake, stolen at that. He meant to cheat yore father out of a fortune."

"But — George? I never cared much about him, but I always thought he was honest."

He listened, nodding. Vance was, indeed a deep rascal. His motives were clear to Hatfield. Vance had figured that if he had plenty of money, which was his god, Edith Voorhees would accept him; thus he would win her father's fortune. Without doubt, Voorhees would have had an "unfortunate accident," once Vance won his first play. Bert Selkirk wouldn't have had a chance, either.

The sheriff was up. "We shore split 'em, Ranger," he cried. "Miss Voorhees, glad to see yuh're okay! And Selkirk, too."

"Take keer of him right off, get him back to Brewster pronto," ordered Hatfield. "I'll be ridin' south."

Davis nodded. "That Mex feller, Don Ramon, said to tell yuh he was goin' on after Vance."

The Ranger's grey-green eyes sought the wild sweep of mountain country to the south. Vance would be driving full-tilt for the Border, trying to reach Mexico and the safety of its jurisdiction. He could hide for years in the fastnesses of the southern republic, maybe never be made to pay for his murderous crimes.

But — if Don Ramon did come up with him, how much chance would the slim young hidalgo, hot-blooded and impetuous to rush into trouble, have against that cunning brain? Could the Mexican cope with Vance? Hatfield shook his head.

Leaving Davis in charge, to see that Selkirk was rushed back to a doctor's care and Edith restored to her frantic father, Hatfield limped along the ledge, his injured leg stiffening up. He found an easy path down to the spot where he had left Goldy.

"Now why'd them two sidewinders try to shin up that cliff?" he mused, staring at the steep rock wall.

The cliffs broke in a series descending to the west. Must be a trail up above, he decided. If he could find a shortcut, he might get down in time to save Don Ramon from Vance. He would head south as Davis's deputies had been sent on to Corellez to clean up.

He climbed up for some distance, and was able to see the faint line of an arroyo leading southward, down past the broken ledges. He could get through that way. Returning to Goldy, he roughly bandaged his leg wound; then he mounted and started through the bush.

It was difficult going for a time, till he

came to that arroyo he had seen. He had to dismount and lead the golden horse at times, but on reaching the dry stream bed he was able to remount and ride along the rocky bottom. His leg held him, though his weight on it was painful.

The arroyo diverged into another deep cut and then he rode along mesquite ridges and down across cactus flats, weaving in and out of the thick brush. The Ranger's long face was grim and grey with pain. He felt that if he lost George Vance, master criminal in this affair, he could not rest easily again.

Before it grew dark, he hit a fairly well-outlined Indian trail. Undoubtedly this was used by Gila Mike's Apaches in hunting deer and stalking through the country.

By moonlight he could slowly keep on heading southward. He rode till Goldy was wearied, then rested till the grey of dawn. The Ranger now traveled on sheer nerve, drawing on the reserves of his mighty system.

The sun was red again when he came to the eastern branch of the trail, the one that led through the canyon of death, where Don Ramon's brother had died. As he hit this path in the wilderness, he noted the fresh hoof marks in the stretches of soft earth.

Crossing the stream near the spot where the Apache Gerajo had tried to creep upon him while he slept that night when he first rode into this wild land, he dismounted to examine the new hoofmarks in the mud. Nostrils flared, eyes narrowed, the Lone Wolf studied these signs. They informed him, as a clearly printed book, about those who had passed.

A man kicks high grass away as he walks, a horse sweeps it back. A horse carrying a rider tends to accentuate the toe impressions, and length of the stride tells the speed. All those things Hatfield could tell at a glance.

It was, however, the leading rider's marks that held him intently. The second track was half superimposed on the other; George Vance was riding ahead, but Don Ramon was pushing along fast on his heels. The impressions of the shoes were slightly different, so Hatfield knew which was Vance's mount. Finding a little farther on another imprint left by Vance's horse, the Ranger noted that the calk of a hind shoe failed to make a dent deeper than the curve.

"Got a busted shoe; when he hits stony ground that pony's apt to lame!" the Ranger said aloud.

He got into his saddle and shoved on,

grim triumph in his heart. Through the chaparral, he rode and, coming at last out on a mesquite-covered summit, looked ahead toward the canyon of death. Several swift black birds were winging westward, away from the trail.

Hoof marks showed that, after crossing a rocky stretch, Vance's mount had gone lame in the hoof to which that broken shoe was nailed. It was as the Ranger had hoped. He was rapidly catching up with his man.

Goldy seemed to sense the end of the long chase and he trotted forward eagerly, nostrils flexed wide in excitement. The Ranger's eyes were fixed ahead on the southern sky as far as he was able to see, looking for warning signs.

Through a vista, he had just a glimpse of the Rio Grande way off below. He saw nothing significant beyond the canyon pass, no birds, no dust that might tell of a rider hurrying through the wilderness.

He dropped down into a depression, spurring forward. Nearing the blind entrance to the canyon, a detached piece of granite-scored mica, gleaming like a galaxy of stars on the sloping face of a great rock deposit, caused him to slow the sorrel.

"Don't like that, Goldy," he muttered.

He heard faintly a shot an instant later,

and the long-drawn out scream of a man, echoing from the death canyon.

Chapter XVIII
The Buzzards Fly!

The Ranger, warned by what he had read in the trail sign, and having divined Vance's play, did not enter the canyon; he dismounted, dropped Goldy's reins to earth, started up the sloping rock face, intending to get up where he could look down on the ledges. His keen ears detected no sounds. Out of sight from below, in a patch of mesquite, stood a lathered, saddled horse. Vance's!

He went silently, hunting each foothold with infinite patience and care, so as not to make any noise. His leg pained, his body ached, his eyes burned for want of sleep, but there was no weakening of his powerful frame. His mind was clear as crystal. High up over the level of those ambush ledges, he crept ahead, six-gun ready in hand.

The piece of mica he had found had told him just what George Vance, riding a fast-laming horse, had planned. Vance had evidently seen something suspicious as he looked back from the heights, realized he was being pursued.

He had swung off before coming to the pass where he had so brutally wiped out the Mexicans, so perfect for ambush, pulled his mount up out of sight of the trail where Hatfield had seen the pony. The animal's hoof had dislodged that piece of mica, enough to warn the keen Ranger.

When Don Ramon, hot on the trail of his brother's murderer, pressed swiftly into the canyon, Vance had shot him. Thus he could obtain an uninjured horse and rid himself of a pursuer.

Hatfield wondered if Vance was aware that there was another close upon him? Hatfield thought he was; the Ranger was counting on that, anyway. No sounds, nothing had come to show that Vance had gone down into the canyon after shooting Acosta. He must be lying up there, waiting for Hatfield.

Now the Ranger, nerves steady, slowly stuck his head up over a flat rock. He could see down on the ledges, and below him a man lay flat on his belly, watching the canyon entrance, a rifle, shaded from the sun by his body, aimed down into the narrow defile. He had a finger on the trigger, and his face was blackly set, fierce, murderous.

It was George Vance, former field man of the Voorhees expedition. "Yuh're shore one cunnin' sidewinder," the Ranger mentally addressed his arch enemy. "Waitin' fer me no doubt of it!"

His six-gun hammer was back under the calloused joint of his long thumb.

Vance was waiting tensely on the ledge, coldly quiet as the death he represented. The Ranger began to work around so that he could descend and catch Vance from a short distance. He meant to take no chances with this man who struck with the efficient, deadly virulence of a killer snake.

Hatfield did not make any noise; no stone rolled under his careful boots. He advanced but a foot or two at a time, keeping as well covered as possible, ignoring the pain from his wounded leg. This stalk took minutes, and George Vance shifted restlessly.

Undoubtedly Vance was becoming suspicious. He possibly was wondering why Hatfield did not come into the canyon, pause to investigate Don Ramon's fallen body, and so die under the rifle without danger to Vance.

Like a wild beast, a stalker himself who senses when he is being stalked, Vance suddenly leaped to his feet and swung full face to Jim Hatfield. His clenched teeth gleamed white, feline under the black smudge of the dude mustache.

Startled, his eyes now shone with red lights of hatred, his real soul exposed in this instant as he saw his implacable foe, Hatfield, the man who had checked and beaten him. But for the Ranger, Vance would have won everything he coveted.

"Reach for the sky and drop that rifle, Vance," the Ranger rapped out.

Hatfield hardly needed to raise his voice, so close were the two men. The incisive order moved Vance as though he had been suddenly stabbed with a sharp needle; his whole body whirled like a panther's and he pulled the trigger of his .30-30 rifle.

The Ranger had raised his thumb an instant before. He felt the tearing impact of Vance's slug, that tore a great chunk from his left arm and then spattered against the rock, smashing it to bits. Staggered, the Lone Wolf fired again as Vance turned and leaped over the edge into the canyon.

Blood was spurting from Hatfield's fresh wound; he was very lame from the leg injury received in the duel with Gila Mike Turner, and greatly weakened by loss of blood and strain.

Through the haze of pain he heard a horse galloping south in the canyon. Had Vance, then, managed to mount Ramon's mustang, start again?

Teeth gritted, oblivious to his pain, and intent only on his enemy, he jumped down to the ledge where Vance had been lying. Now he could see into the canyon. Below him lay Don Ramon Acosta, helpless, staring up at the narrow ribbon of blue sky. A second body, doubled on its side, sprawled within a few feet of the Mexican. It was George Vance.

Hatfield sent a bullet so close to Vance that it burned through the man's shirt, and would have forced him to twitch had he been conscious; but Vance stayed quiet. It was Ramon's pony which had run, saddle empty, out of the canyon when Vance had plunged from his ledge.

The Lone Wolf, biting his lip to keep the agony of his wounds under control, made his way down into the bloody pass. He limped to Vance, gun up, still wary of a trap. Vance was capable of anything, but, coming to the lean body, he saw how well he had made his shot as Vance had leaped.

The slug had smashed through the back of Vance's head and torn away half the skull-pan as it emerged. Vance had been dead before he hit the rocks, among the whitened skeletons of his massacre victims. His face, in death, was twisted into a fiendish expression, showing the fierce nature which he had hidden behind his smooth exterior.

The Ranger sat down beside Don Ramon Acosta. The Mexican gave a low moan and shifted. Hatfield inspected his friend. Vance's slug had narrowly missed the Mexican's vitals; it had smashed his shoulder and the bloody froth on his lips indicated his lung had been punctured. Ramon coughed weakly.

Hatfield painfully limped the distance to Goldy. He had a flask of brandy in his warsack, and he rode the golden sorrel back to Acosta, poured fiery liquid between the pallid lips.

After a time, Don Ramon returned to consciousness. His breathing was raspy but his gaze softened as he looked up at the stern faced American.

"So — you came. *Si,* I knew you would," he whispered. "I rode swiftly after him, Vance, murderer of Luis and my people. I start' soon as I meet Sheriff Davis, and gave heem your orders. Where ees he, I mean Vance, killer of my brother?"

"Kin yuh turn yore haid a little?"

Ramon's eyes swung, fastened on the cruel, death-twisted face of George Vance. A smile played around the Mexican's aristocratic mouth.

"Gracias," he murmured — "Thanks, a thousand thanks!"

"Wonder has he got that ransom money on him?" muttered Hatfield. "He shore come close to gittin' away, Ramon. Was haidin' for safety. We got no jurisdiction in Mexico. Vance jest crossed all his men cold and lit out with the cash. He's 'bout as foxy a devil as ever I crossed guns with. Mebbe I'll miss him — he kept me from gittin' overslept at night!"

Hatfield limped over, set about searching the corpse of his crafty opponent. Vance wore no belts under his clothing and had but a few dollars in his pockets.

Puzzled, the Ranger rested again, studying the situation and then went over to Vance's mount. Having solved a vexing problem, Jim Hatfield started on his way to Brewster.

Sheriff Davis and his posse met Jim Hatfield pushing Goldy north from the canyon of death. Don Ramon was strapped on the back of the lame pony that could walk, though he limped from a strained tendon caused by a broken horseshoe calk.

The big Ranger sat erect in his saddle. There were bulky places, one on his leg, another on the stiffened left arm, roughly bandaged, but he was still riding. As they came in sight of the party from Brewster, Goldy gave a neigh that was a boast of victory.

"Okay," Hatfield replied shortly to the flurry of questions Davis put. "Yuh'll find Voorhees' money in them saddlebags on Vance's pony. And Acosta here will survive."

"And Vance — did he git away?"

The majestic power of the great Lone Wolf always awed men, but it was never so keenly felt as at that moment. He was as calm as the blue wilderness sky, which he indicated by a sweep of his arm, as he turned in his saddle.

High in that sky black specks were plummeting down, swooping on the canyon of death. The *caracaras,* the saturnine Mexican vultures, were dropping for their ghastly feast.

Davis slapped a chap-covered thigh. "Yessir," he murmured admiringly, "when a lone wolf like him prowls, the buzzards shore fly!"

There was sweeping-up to be done, in Corellez and Brewster. Jim Hatfield assisted and, having finished his great job, Goldy and he headed back east, back to Ranger Headquarters where Cap'n Bill McDowell waited.

It was a fair, blue-skied morning when Jim Hatfield walked in. Silently he saluted his superior, the man who had despatched him on his mission.

"Brewster is clean," Hatfield reported succinctly as he remained standing before the older man.

McDowell's gnarled old brows came together. For a time he did not speak, simply looked at the mighty young man who stood there before him. There was huge affection and understanding between the two, a feeling so deep that it could not be expressed.

As steely McDowell looked at Jim Hatfield he was glad that the job was behind. But, there was a harsh note in McDowell's voice when he spoke.

"Well," he asked, "did yuh stamp out that ME Connected rustlin'?"

"Yes sir. Won't be no more — not by the same parties, anyways."

"Run into any trouble?" McDowell enjoyed probing this tight-lipped man for information.

"A little," Hatfield replied looking off into space.

"Dawggone, he shore don't b'lieve in wastin' words," thought McDowell.

He had heard the repercussions all the

way from Brewster, for Sheriff Davis had sent him a communication. Nor had he missed Hatfield's slight limp as the Lone Wolf came into the office. He had also seen the fresh bullet sears on the officer's bronzed hide.

"I hear," drawled Cap'n Bill, "yuh sorta ripped up a mushroom town called Corellez."

"Yessir. One George Vance worked out a crooked plan to cheat a rich hombre named Voorhees by sellin' him some fake Aztec stuff. The other crimes follered out of that. Davis done got a hundred bandit pris'ners; and silver trinkets stolen from a Mex pack-train returned to the owners."

There was a little tightness in the older man's voice as he came to the point uppermost in his mind.

"And — what about Ranger Martin?"

Silently Hatfield reached into his pocket and took out the silver star set on a silver circle, the Ranger badge that he had recovered from Dude. This had been the badge that had been used in freeing Gila Mike from the jail in Brewster.

Hatfield held it in his cupped hand for a moment; he looked down at it as if he were making anew all the vows of strength and integrity that made the Lone Star law what

229

it stood for. Quietly he laid the silver emblem on McDowell's desk.

"That second Ranger," Hatfield said huskily, "was one of Vance's gunmen. But Vance stabbed Martin to death."

McDowell's fists tightened, his nails digging into the horny palms of his hands. "Yuh arrested this Vance skunk?"

Hatfield shook his head. "He wouldn't arrest, Cap'n," he drawled.

McDowell understood perfectly. He did not need to see the buzzards circling in the sky to realize that George Vance had paid for his crimes.

Picking up Martin's star, he rubbed his thumb over it and stared at it.

"I'll keep it," he muttered, "keep it as a reminder of what happens to them who dare kill a Ranger."

Placing the badge in his inner coat pocket horny-handed Bill McDowell put away from sight one of his sorest hurts — a Ranger slain. Deep in him there was a sadness that neither revenge, nor death, could heal.

To the man who sat behind the wide oak desk and sent men on missions that meant certain death or glory, there was a greater humanity. He felt that the loss of one of them was a great price. But law there must be!

As he looked at Jim Hatfield he noticed the drawn lines around his mouth. He noticed also that the Lone Wolf stood with one knee bent.

"Mebbe yuh need a rest, Hatfield. Yuh've had a long ride and a dangerous one, from what I hear. There's still tall trouble over yonder, and yuh're the man for the job, but —"

Hatfield straightened up, grey-green eyes alight and flickering.

"We're ready," the Lone Wolf said, "ready to ride, Cap'n."

McDowell chuckled inwardly. He'd known what Hatfield's answer would be. This young Texan was the apple of his eye, his greatest lawman. But the trail would keep.

"Not this time, Hatfield," he said, shaking his head. "Not until yuh can stand on that leg, stretch that arm."

Hatfield's face flushed. "Well," he said slowly, "the only thing for me and Goldy to do is to go find some tall grass and stay still till yuh call me."

Hatfield saluted and went out to the sorrel. Cap'n Bill watched him turn, ride off again, this time to become fit to carry Texas law to the violent wilds of the Southwest.

"The man ain't born yit who can beat him," he muttered.

The dry dust whirled up under Goldy's beating hoofs as the sorrel carried his mighty master toward the tall grass. Soon the Lone Wolf would ride sign on killers whose guns barked doom for their own evil handlers by calling down on their heads the power of the Rangers.